HUNTED

OUTRUN. OUTLAST. OUTWIT.

Tales Of Discovery

Edited By Kat Cockrill

First published in Great Britain in 2020 by:

Young Writers
Remus House
Coltsfoot Drive
Peterborough
PE2 9BF
Telephone: 01733 890066
Website: www.youngwriters.co.uk

Book Design by Ashley Janson

Softback ISBN 978-1-83928-828-9

Printed and bound in the UK by BookPrintingUK
Website: www.bookprintinguk.com
YB0436P

FOREWORD

IF YOU'VE BEEN SEARCHING FOR EPIC ADVENTURES, TALES OF SUSPENSE AND IMAGINATIVE WRITING THEN SEARCH NO MORE! YOUR HUNT IS AT AN END WITH THIS ANTHOLOGY OF MINI SAGAS.

We challenged secondary school students to craft a story in just 100 words. In this first installment of our SOS Sagas, their mission was to write on the theme of 'Hunted'. But they weren't restricted to just predator vs prey, oh no. They were encouraged to think beyond their first instincts and explore deeper into the theme.

The result is a variety of styles and genres and, as well as some classic cat and mouse games, inside these pages you'll find characters looking for meaning, people running from their darkest fears or maybe even death itself on the hunt.

Here at Young Writers it's our aim to inspire the next generation and instill in them a love for creative writing, and what better way than to see their work in print? The imagination and skill within these pages are proof that we might just be achieving that aim! Well done to each of these fantastic authors.

So if you're ready to find out if the hunter will become the hunted, read on!

CONTENTS

THE STORIES

Operation Chimera

The police car sirens wailed as the helicopter buzzed overhead. Five loud thuds echoed around the small town. Weapons drawn, the operators rushed down the apocalyptical street. The Chimera virus destroyed everything in its wake. Groan. The weapons lit up.
Inside the hot springs resort, the operators laid nano-thermite charges while fending off the impending disaster. Aliens used humans hosts.
Rushing out of the barbecued resort, the operators watched as their helicopter dropped from the sky, blades slowing. "Jager! No!" Doc screamed down the radio as the helicopter hit the gas station. Their transport was gone. They were alone.

Rohan Phillips (13)
Aldercar High School, Langley Mill

Hunting The Evil

I picked up my rifle and started running after the traitor. The traitor of evil started running for dear life and he heard a gunshot. He got hit right in the head. He got captured and was taken to my torture house. He got strapped to my machine which stretches their shins. "Argh, the torture is too bad! Please stop this! Please, I'm begging you!"
"Okay, on one condition... stop telling my secrets!"
"Never!"
"Well, it's time to die..."
"I dare you to even try! You'll fail!"
"I don't think so..." With one shot, he died.

James Wood (13)
Aldercar High School, Langley Mill

Run, Run, Run, Run, Survive, Survive, Survive, Survive

Run, run, run, run, survive, survive, survive, survive. He awoke late one night. What's this? He couldn't move. He looked down to see a strange figure at the foot of his bed. It muttered, "Run, run, run, run, survive, survive, survive, survive..." Then the figure left. Alarmed, he struggled to get back to sleep.

Days after it, there was a strange feeling everywhere he went. A crazy sensation. Like he was being... watched. He thought nothing of it but then he remembered the thing's muttered words. *Run, run, run, run, survive, survive, survive, survive...* So, that's what he did.

Evie Gallagher (12)

Aldercar High School, Langley Mill

Last Recordings

Audio Log: 7am GMT 11th October 2020.
I still have nightmares about it. A whole twenty-four hours and I still failed. My mistake has cost the world and I'm the only one who got off it, leaving the other seven billion to die in an atomic fireball. The Earth will be uninhabitable for millennia, unless something out there is radiation-proof. My food and water will run out eventually. It's ironic that after escaping a nuclear war, I'm going to die by something simple like starving to death. Unfortunate really.

Audio Log: 9:30pm GMT 13th December 2020.
They are coming.

Thomas Wright (13)
Aldercar High School, Langley Mill

They Are Coming

Eleven at night, the sirens wailed. It was time to leave. They were in the rooftops. Scouting. It wasn't safe now. I shouldn't have done it. They had no chance. The apocalypse was upon us. Memories surrounded me. They were getting close... too close. I saw a bike. I ran for it. So did they. Shots were fired. Luckily, I won. The bike purred. I was off down the road then, out of nowhere, they appeared, as if they were invisible. "Stop! It's over!" I stopped. They walked over, smiled and congratulated me. "Welcome to the Force... partner!"

Ethan Paver-Brown (13)
Aldercar High School, Langley Mill

Never Go Into The Forest

This very dark night, the blue moon started to rise, lighting the sky. The wolves followed the blue moon's rays. I could hear their paws approaching. I could also hear the trees rattling, shaking. I started breathing rapidly, my legs were shaking, my heart was pounding. As I watched them, they began to transform into werewolves. I ran as fast as I could. I reached the forest as the werewolves grabbed my leg. I felt their sharp teeth pierce my skin... blood trickled everywhere. I made it into the house, the werewolves scratching the door, ripping it apart... Fear.

Wesley Marchant (15)
Aldercar High School, Langley Mill

Creature Of The Deep

A vicious roar from beneath, followed by the ship cracking in two. What was a mining operation quickly turned into a rescue mission. I bolted through the hull. This thing's tentacles were sharper than knives, piercing the engines to our submarine. I made a sharp turn right, hallway 6-E, towards the life pods. All I heard was beeping, loud shouting and power fluctuations. I grabbed the hatch and leapt in, forwarding all power to thrust. I shot into the sky with an emergency beacon. It was below me, that thing was bigger than New York, bigger than a Leviathan.

Ewen Thomas Fillingham (15)
Aldercar High School, Langley Mill

The House Fire

We had to leave. Now. Now or never. The house burning down, ablaze, the fiery, rising flames crawling up the walls. My life flashed before me. What will happen if I die? "Burn in Hell!" the voice of fire screamed. I bashed through the wooden door and slid down the polished bannister which reflected the flames behind. I scurried through the key box and latched onto the house key, my fingers trembling, my body shaking. I pushed the key into the lock, twisted it and ran out the door. Wait. Where's my brother? I've... I've just killed him.

Joseph Davis (14)
Aldercar High School, Langley Mill

The Traitor

I was close. I needed him. I needed Alexios. He was a Spartan traitor to Leonidas. He had vital information on the dreaded shield wall and how to break it. I arrived. How many Spartan soldier's heads were on spikes? I needed to kill him. There he was, the traitor, the king's guard. He raised his sword. The fight commenced. He was a legend, a god. I sliced him, dodged, then stabbed him. Alexios was dead. I picked up the blade he had used to murder so many people. Engraved on the blade, it said, *Kill. Survive. Become Leonida's successor.*

Dylan Colborne (12)
Aldercar High School, Langley Mill

The Unknown Reality

I still have nightmares about it, waking up at unusual times, my heart pounding like elephant footsteps. A crack in the branches like my eyes burning into shrinking peas. Shivering arms reach for my duvet, hiding in it like it's my only protection. Heavy eyes, slowly falling asleep. Running away from a strange place where chemicals are made, ripping plastic tubes that are stuck into my furry skin, sirens chasing me. Racing now, my ears pricked up, heard gunshots. Green smoke everywhere. I can hardly see. My breath paused in fear. Will they find me?

Jordi Green
Aldercar High School, Langley Mill

Eater Of Souls

The sky soon faded to black. The fiery glow illuminated the forest before being absorbed by the darkness. I peered through the towering trees, trembling with fear. I could feel an evil presence watching my every move. I scurried like a mouse to the chasm entrance. I climbed down, hoping to not fall into the abyss. Finally, I made it to the bottom and scanned the area, my eyes still adjusting to the darkness. I could hear the scraping of claws on rocks. Suddenly, I was lifted from the ground. It stared deep into my soul, its eyes illuminated purple.

Leo Goodrum (13)
Aldercar High School, Langley Mill

The Story Of Ezmai-Jay!

Sirens blazing, I ran over the hills and through the leech-filled waters until I reached a school, abandoned, aged by time. Surreptitiously, I went in but, instantly, it was no longer abandoned. There were people everywhere, not just normal people. People with superpowers. There were kids with laser eyes and freeze breath! A teacher came running towards me. Terror crossed my mind. They asked me where I came from. I told them I had escaped from an asylum because I was able to shoot fire out of my hands. They gasped and welcomed me to their school!

Elie-Mai Pearson (15)
Aldercar High School, Langley Mill

Stranded

They locked me up. It's because I'm alien. I just want to go home. I mean no harm. I escaped but I'm not sure how. Everything is blurry. I just know I'm running, sprinting away from Hell. Terror pushes me forwards. My glowing blue skin illuminates the silent, gloomy forest around me. Dry leaves crunch under my bare feet. They are still hunting me. I can hear them calling for me. I need my ship. Even if I get to it, home is light-years away. I stopped suddenly, collapsing to my shaking knees. I was stranded here. Forever alone.

Summer Donson (13)
Aldercar High School, Langley Mill

Escape Day

I awoke in my prison cell. *Today is escape day.* Without being seen, I took my knife (that I took from the cafeteria) and moved my poster to see a large hole in the wall. Finally, I was out. I started running. Suddenly, the alarm rang. It got louder, like it was chasing me. I sprinted through the bushes and splashed through the muddy, unclear river. Dogs! Their growl sent shivers down my spine. I couldn't stop or return. Forward called to me. I was lost. A deep ravine lurked ahead of me. I couldn't go back. I was surrounded.

Jake Antony Quimby (12)
Aldercar High School, Langley Mill

Perfection

I couldn't run for much longer. Surely it couldn't have followed us this far? We slowed to a walk and heard the distinctive, robotic voice. "You shall become perfect!" We would have to summon the strength to move on. Us, the three survivors, the only hope. There was no way to the invaders. Wave after wave came, each one longer, each one stronger. We hung by a strand of hope, hope of survival. Suddenly, headlights lit up the road. They had found us. All around were the words 'perfection' hanging thick in the air. We were to become perfect.

Sam Cooper (12)
Aldercar High School, Langley Mill

Eyes

Long ago in an old cemetery, two children found an old doll.
They left it on the wall and went home.
When they got home they went to their room and they saw the doll sat on the shelf! They threw it out the window. Then they made a huge mistake. They fell asleep.
One of them woke and saw something blood-curdling. Her friend was lying on the floor, her eyes pulled out and a knife through her chest.
"Run," she whispered. Then she died.
They say the doll is still out there searching for her next doomed victim...

Ellen Moore
Aldercar High School, Langley Mill

The Masked Man

It's not safe now. He knows. He's found me. The masked man from my childhood. The nightmare of my life who murdered my dreams and brought out my dark side. He was following me in the dark depths of the streets. I wanted to turn around but I couldn't. I wanted to run but I couldn't. Behind me, I felt like the masked man was watching my every move as the figure wrenched closer. I couldn't move. I was frozen to the spot. I couldn't scream because my mouth was taped shut. Footsteps behind me got louder and louder...

Rachel Parr (11)
Aldercar High School, Langley Mill

Running

The sirens blared out, the beasts were let free. You could hear the vicious growls of the bloodthirsty dogs from miles away as the sound echoed loudly and lights flickered through the dark woods. My arm was bleeding from the bite of the dog. If I didn't stop it soon, it would be my demise. The guards were chasing and catching up to me. It wouldn't be long until they caught me. After an hour of running in the freezing weather in the pitch-black night, the prison guards called the search off. Everything went white. It was over...

Sam Edward Whitaker (13)
Aldercar High School, Langley Mill

Ready Or Not, Here I Come!

My heart is beating uncontrollably. I can't breathe. I feel a tear slowly run down my cheek, my legs shaking. Whatever it is, it's getting closer. "Ready or not, here I come..." My heart stops, my whole body paralysed. It comes from the dark corner of the room. I'm trying to run but I can't move. I try screaming but all that comes out is a small, timid gasp. I feel something heavy and cold on my shoulders, it's grabbing me tighter and tighter. It giggles and then whispers, "Found you!"
"Ugh, okay. I'll count this time, Emily!"

Jessica Fuller (13)
Aldercar High School, Langley Mill

The Explosive

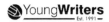

"Damn! They're right behind me. Oh yeah, I have flares!" Footsteps came to a halt after a mix of fiery orange and red shot into the air. "Now's my chance!" I ran, ran for my life. This... disease has taken everything from me. Now I'm going to take everything from these things. Not that they had anything to lose. Wait, I can hear them. "So, you finally decided to show up. Took you a while. Hey, what are you screaming at? Oh... you want the explosive?" I removed the pin, "Not much longer. You want the explosive? Well, go fetch!"

Archie Whelan (12)
Aldercar High School, Langley Mill

We Are Not Safe, They Are Coming!

We have to leave now before the parasite infects us. If we want to make it out alive, we will have to work together. First things first, we need to build a shelter, then we need to get weapons to defend ourselves. We have named the parasite, The Destroyer because it turns you into a monster and you lose control. I can't run for much longer before I become one of them and infect the entire world.
One year later, I still have nightmares about what happened on that day. I'm glad I found the antidote to cure them.

Jack Blanchard (12)
Aldercar High School, Langley Mill

We're The Supernaturals

I heard the siren wailing endlessly behind me, getting quieter as I continued onwards. I'd become even more of a target to them than I already was, all in the space of a few seconds. But, there wasn't any other option. I could either surrender and be rid of my life as a consequence or die trying to regain justice for all of us. If I dared to look back, I'd be shot dead in an instant. That's what they do to people like me. We're different and, to them, that means we're dangerous. They're not wrong. We're the supernaturals.

Chloe Hallam (12)
Aldercar High School, Langley Mill

Survival

I couldn't run for much longer. I'd been running for miles. My legs were throbbing. My heart was pounding but I couldn't stop. They would find me otherwise. The odds were against me. I had no food, no water, no shelter. I wouldn't let them catch me if my life depended on it. Every limb was either bruised or broken but this was for my family. I was determined to survive this. The overgrown path seemed to go on forever. My pain and my anger were what kept me going. I just wanted them to feel what I felt.

Leah Dalton Thawley (14)
Aldercar High School, Langley Mill

Inner Demons

I can't hide for much longer. They will find me and when they do, they will kill me... Everybody makes mistakes. I've had more than my share, to be honest. I didn't mean to summon it. Summoning demons is a definite no-no, okay? Never ever under any circumstances do you summon a demon. I can hear it now. The clippity-clop of its hooves as it slowly advances towards my hiding spot. I hold my breath, tensing up as it stops millimetres away from me. I see its smile, its jagged, yellow teeth, its red eyes...

Lily Mae Thomas
Aldercar High School, Langley Mill

My Last Breath

I couldn't run for much longer. The thing was following me. The more steps I took, the quicker my breath went. I couldn't hear, I couldn't move. I couldn't breathe. Things appeared all around me. I couldn't stop thinking. *Bang!* Here it came... the unknown creature creeping upon me as I took my final breath of air... or, what I thought was my last breath. The minute the malevolent thing could get its claws on me, I ran, not knowing where I was going to end up or if I was going to live.

Isabel Stack (12)
Aldercar High School, Langley Mill

Possessed

When I was eleven, your great grandfather told me a story and now I'll tell it to you. There was once a book that, if you opened it, it would let out all the spirits and your nightmares became reality. As I became fourteen, I thought about being a ghost hunter, so I started to study some ghost books. But, the last book I looked at was actually the Book of Spirits and, without me knowing, I released the spirits. As I was stopped by a creature, I ran dramatically. Unfortunately, it turned out I was the hunted.

Jack Searson (11)
Aldercar High School, Langley Mill

The Dream Job

A pack of wolves still kept their scent on me. Somehow. Suddenly, sirens wailed. I knew what to do. I grabbed my rifle from my backpack, turned around and shot once. All of them changed into dust. It was a hologram. "Training completed student 557. You are now one of us!" The colonel turned around and gave me a little wink. I got escorted to the back room where I was given my uniform and some glasses that could blow up the universe. I finally did it. I got my dream job. My dad was going to be very proud.

Harry Thomas Paget (12)
Aldercar High School, Langley Mill

It's Not Safe

It wasn't safe, they knew what I was. Police were raiding my house, looking for me. I trembled in fear. I never thought this would happen, at least not to me. There were more of us, so I needed to warn them. I scurried across the floor and then flew away as fast as a rabbit running from a predator. They wouldn't know I was disguised as a seagull. I went to base. When I arrived, I transformed myself again. They had been found and taken and so had I. They took me away. I never lived another day.

Lexie Stapleton-Bojko
Aldercar High School, Langley Mill

The Critters

It crawled towards me like a small scorpion but this was 100 times bigger with its venomous fangs dripping with venom. I was hung up in a web, it went in circles around me. I pulled the small, 9mm gun from my pocket and shot the critter and escaped from the web. Her babies opened up their egg sack and chased me. I shot so many with the pistol but they doubled when they died. There were at least 400 of them now. "Over here!" As someone got eaten alive by the small spiders, I jumped on a helicopter.

Kyle Longdon (11)
Aldercar High School, Langley Mill

Run

I had to leave now. Every time I saw his decaying face and bruises and blistered hands. I had to go. I could hear the crunch of the leaves. My heavy breathing. I didn't dare look back. I had to hide. I jumped behind the nearest log. I was safe. For now. I tried to muffle my terrified screams but when he came back, I couldn't hold it back. I woke up as I saw him staring with a blank expression as he opened his face into a horrifying beast. He walked closer and closer until it got to me...

Logan Gettle (11)
Aldercar High School, Langley Mill

The Hidden Creature Of The Night

It was midnight and I was in my room, reading Harry Potter, when I heard someone scratching on my wall. Well, I thought it was someone. I got out of my bed to see who it was. I looked up because I saw a shadow-type creature. I turned. Then blacked out.

I woke up hours later in a ditch. I saw a pair of claw-like hands scratching the floor. Then, two glowing red eyes looked at me. I said hello but all I got was something thrown at me. I looked closely. It was a dead stag skeleton.

William C N Worthington (11)
Aldercar High School, Langley Mill

Run Away

The sirens wailed in my ears, my legs burnt and my lungs ached but I couldn't stop. I could never stop. The sirens slowly faded into the distance. I had nowhere to go. I started walking along the side of the road. Every time a car went by, I dove into a ditch. Then I heard the sirens. How had they found me? I had to hide. I ran into an abandoned house. I found a secret compartment and hid in it. I heard them approach me. They opened it and everything went dark. They had found me.

Dylan Cooper (12)
Aldercar High School, Langley Mill

The Apocalypse

I couldn't run for much longer. They were after me. The apocalypse had started. The end was near. It wasn't much longer before I would become a citizen of the afterlife. The flesh-eating zombies were quicker than I thought. I had run as fast as my legs could carry me but using all my strength, I lost my breath. The meat-eating cannibals sped up and, before I knew it, they caught up to me. I felt the dagger-like teeth shred up my skin. I had become a cannibalised zombie.

Heather Stovin (11)
Aldercar High School, Langley Mill

Alien Chase

I couldn't run for any longer as I thought my imagination was getting to me. An alien was chasing me in the dark. My tears flew back into the midnight wind. I hid in a small box, locking myself inside, holding my breath. Then, I heard a loud knock and kick. As the door swung open, I couldn't believe it, an actual alien was chasing me down a street at midnight. I slapped my face to see if it was a dream but the alien had got me for good. No way of escaping him now at night.

Megan Harris (12)
Aldercar High School, Langley Mill

Hide-And-Seek

I kept searching. My sharp knife was clutched in my right hand as I walked through the kaleidoscopic maze. Bright lights shone in my eyes, making me squint with an evil smile plastered on my bloodstained face. Saliferous blood trickled down my forehead. I turned a corner and caught sight of someone in one of the many mirrors. "Hide-and-seek, here I come..." I whispered to myself before proceeding, euphoria running through me, my smile growing wider.

Heather Islay Eldred (12)
Aldercar High School, Langley Mill

End Of Eternity

I stopped dead. My head was pounding and I couldn't believe what I had just gone through. Two cars had literally just skidded around the corner and crashed. I just ran away from the facility and I was out of breath. Police cars came racing around and I tried to think of good ideas. I climbed up a building. My foot slipped but I managed to stay upwards. I carried on climbing. Suddenly, I fell, my whole body stopped.

Toby Torr (11)
Aldercar High School, Langley Mill

Run

The sirens walked as I ran. They were after me. I didn't even steal anything. I ran around the corner. "What do they think I've done?" I said to myself. They were back after me. I started to run again. I couldn't run for much longer. As I thought I got away, I did.
As I was heading home, my friend pulled up to me on his bike and said, "You're wanted, you know?"
What?

Alfie Pearson (11)
Aldercar High School, Langley Mill

The Invasion

The sirens wailed. As I ran out of the back of the store, I was caught. Trying my best to get away, I made my way to the park but got trapped against the brick wall. But, that's when it happened. My eyes adjusted to the light from the sudden flash and the officers were gone. What was going to happen? Everything went black. I heard a *zoom!* It was morning again. The sirens were back.

Joshua Canlin
Aldercar High School, Langley Mill

Hunted

I'm still having nightmares about it. It was almost a year ago. Here's what happened. I was just walking my dog down the street when, all of a sudden, this person in a black suit attacked me and pushed me to the ground. I was so scared, I didn't dare move or make a sound but the next thing I knew, I was kidnapped and put in this basement but I managed to escape.

Millie Bednall (11)
Aldercar High School, Langley Mill

SML Movie: Jeffy's Diamond

I couldn't run any longer. The English Secret Service, they thought I'd stolen a diamond the size of a whiteboard. I had twenty-four hours to escape. If I was cool, I would make a YouTube video but I was not. I heard something in the distance so I drove to the airport to fly to America. Hopefully, the FBI doesn't catch me. The sirens wailed...

George Nugent (12)
Aldercar High School, Langley Mill

Killer On The Loose

It was a late evening and in the deep, dark alley, a crowd of men gathered and bellowed, "Forest! Forest!" But, out of nowhere, a crowd of Rams fans arrived and chanted, "Derby! Derby! Derby!" Unexpectedly, a gunshot was fired from the Forest fans, then the killer ran. The Rams chased and chased. The killer was on the loose.

Liam Derbyshire (11)
Aldercar High School, Langley Mill

On The Run

The sirens wailed in the distance; I didn't have much time. They said I wouldn't get caught. After the bank job, there was nowhere to go. They were close now. Snapping sticks echoed through the derelict forest. The sacred forest. A deafening silence struck the forest. Gasping, freezing, hiding, I ducked behind a monstrous stump. Blinding flashlights illuminated the woodland. Loud shouts and even barks reverberated and rebounded off trees. "Come out with your hands up!" boomed a voice above me. A massive light lit up the forest. The tracker! They knew! Wait! I had experience! I could disable it!

Ingmarr Mark (14)
Harris CE Academy, Bilton

Run For Your Life

I couldn't run for much longer. My legs burn in absolute agony as I dash my way through the thick, befound mud. Bitter cold creeping down the tips of my fingers, my heart thumping out of my chest like a drum. Blood oozing out my leg from the sharp, knife-like claws of this creature. Suddenly, everything went silent, all I could hear were my darkest thoughts. A horrifying scream struck me. My whole body went stone-cold. Frozen in fear, waiting for the moment I was going to die. My vision going blurry from the agonising pain. Darkness engulfing me.

Erin Lorelle Burke (14)
Harris CE Academy, Bilton

The Beginning Of The End

We had to leave. Now. Sprinting through back alleys of this dystopian, 2050 city was difficult since somewhat most of it was in ruins. Tyrannical narcissists ran the country and had not cared for it. The bomb was to be launched and dropped at three in the afternoon. We ran the instant the news flash came on. *Wail! Wail! Wail! Wail!* Sirens blared. Screams could be heard over the top of them. If the leaders wanted survivors, they would have pre-warned us. They didn't. They needed to get rid of us and now it was too late for us all.

Sam McCullough (15)
Harris CE Academy, Bilton

Sweet Silence

Crashing through the window, I watched as the rogue, wild shard of glass pierced my skin and cut my Achilles heel. I lay there in a pool of my own blood, unable to move, paralysed by fear, my thoughts racing as I heard the sound of twigs snapping like bones, one by one, growing faster second by second until one final one. For a second, there was nothing, it was peaceful until the wild juggernaut burst through the rotted wall, blowtorch flaming in hand. As he stopped over me with his barbaric, savage eyes, I felt vulnerable then sweet silence.

Owen Nelson (15)
Harris CE Academy, Bilton

The Unknown

We have to leave, now. Screaming, yelling, roaring came from the pitch-black corridor. I slammed the door shut and locked it. I knew it wouldn't hold them forever. I looked around worriedly for an object that would obliterate the window to pieces. I saw something shine from the corner of the torn-apart room. I picked up the tiny, smooth rock and lunged it at the window, smashing it into millions of pieces. I leapt out of the window not knowing what was below me. I closed my eyes and hoped for the best. I landed but then they surrounded me.

Miles Copperwheat (14)
Harris CE Academy, Bilton

Farmland

Old, derelict, decaying, my house stood on antique farmland. I was playing underground when I heard a shot through the portal that led to the outside. I was in shock and I couldn't move as he shot all of my family members. I heard the supersonic screams of rain downstairs. I heard him coming downstairs, the squeak of the stairs sent shivers down my back. He kicked open the antique door of my room, light streaming into the darkened room, sending shadows dashing to the darkened corners. As the light shone upon me, darkness swallowed me.

Ramon Rudans
Harris CE Academy, Bilton

The Run

We had to leave, now. He had disappeared for twenty-four hours. We had the chance to make a run for it into the woods behind the disused, derelict, dangerous outhouse. The door was left unlocked. All we could smell was humid, tense, fresh air. Sprinting, stumbling, we made our way into the woods but we heard a loud engine pulling up. "Run!" we said, galloping as quick as we could go. Turning around, we couldn't see the house anymore. It had vanished, nowhere to be seen. It had gone, vanished into thin air. Gone for good.

Freya Jenkins (15)
Harris CE Academy, Bilton

The Escape

The sirens wailed as I leapt over the gigantic wall. Shrieking, roaring, screeching, the radios called out for me, hungrily. I couldn't escape them. As I fled the scene, I saw millions of police running after me, beasts who were after my freedom. Sprinting for the SWAT van, I gasped for breath as my lungs drowned in agony. I couldn't escape the feeling of anxiety consuming me, scopes locked on my head. The searchlights beamed as they blazed through the car park like a fire consuming me I gazed at the mile-long road, waiting...

Jordan Garratt (14)
Harris CE Academy, Bilton

Hunted

I couldn't run for much longer. They were after me but it wasn't my fault. "It was him!" I said but they didn't listen and... *bang!* They shot. They tried to shoot me! But missed. They were terrible shots. But I ran so fast for so long that my legs had become dead. My lungs were still alive, they burnt with fire. My ribs ached and my uvula felt like it was being stabbed with shards of glass because of the icy wind. But they came after me, hunting me down and they were never going to stop. Never.

Georgeja Bradshaw (14)
Harris CE Academy, Bilton

The Time Has Come

We were close. As I dashed, the sweat wrinkled my fingers as if I had aged thirty years. As I looked back, I saw a splatter of red and chunks of meat fly from what used to be a boy's head but I had to go on. *Bang! Clap! Screech!* The cacophony of horseshoes clapping on the stone pavement and whistles of lawmen as they screamed, calling us to a halt. Splats of chunky, red blotches leaked onto the pavement like paint thrown onto a blank canvas and we could already feel the hangman's noose around all our necks.

Ewan McNaughton (14)
Harris CE Academy, Bilton

I Still Remember

I still remember that day on the 3rd June 1940. I had twenty-four hours to defeat the Germans, pushing them out of Dunkirk. I led two pilots, Nathan and Daniel, with me. Flying over the ocean, we saw ships set out to pick up our men. Suddenly, bombs went off in the corner of my eye. I saw two bombers, so we flanked left, following them and when we were in range, we fired, taking them out and crashing. Reinforcements came and we started attacking the bombers on the beach so they fled and I went back home for dinner.

Leon Attwell (14)
Harris CE Academy, Bilton

The Shadow Awakens

As the dark night covered the sky, the freezing wind crawled over my shivering body. Trees surrounded the vast, secluded area. *This might be the last day I live!* My legs collapsed beneath me. A dark, mysterious figure emerged from the shadows; *is it them?* He slowly edged towards me. His footsteps matched the pace of my increasing heart rate. A bullet flew past my cheek, burning the skin off its smooth surface. As I turned my head not a single trace of a person was there. A bright beam of light hit my eyes - my time had come.

Jevonte Raymond (14)
Impact Independent School, Dudley

Always There

Fast, fast, even faster I run. Everywhere I go, it follows. Blood trails here and there. I can't get away from this... thing... not in my head or in my reality. It's there; always there. I crouch and hide. I think I see it for a split second. Sharp, pointed teeth, dripping thick, crimson blood. Dead, lifeless eyes and an evil grin. As soon as I see it, it disappears. A sharp pain punctures my chest. I grab at the pain. Blood slips away from me... my life slips away from me... *it* stays with me.

Jake Pedley (14)
Impact Independent School, Dudley

Back To The Asylum

As the fearful night falls upon us, the hunting begins. I have to prepare. I sharpen my blade when sound makes my heart race; my pulse elevates dramatically. I turn. A laser is pointing directly at my head. My mind says run; my body won't move. "E45Q! Come back before we shoot!" As the last words left his mouth I had a sudden burst of adrenaline and ran. My muscles strained; I had the speed of a cheetah. The formula has worked. I can't go back... to the asylum. I must find a way back to my own planet.

Taite Brooks (14)

Impact Independent School, Dudley

Prey

The darkness flickered, maybe it was just an illusion. The branches stroked my bare skin as I trudged onwards in the deadly darkness. My prey was almost in my grasp but, as yet, she didn't know it. I felt the sharpness of the blade pierce my skin. The smell of fresh blood made my adrenalin race. I considered my next move. Suddenly everything went blank. I dropped to the forest floor. The last thing I saw was a rock in her hand and her evil smile in the moonlight. The hunter had become the hunted.

Joshua Smith (14)
Impact Independent School, Dudley

Killer

I see a glimmer of light in the distance. I see my prey and I begin to run faster. I begin the hunt. The animal is fast; not as fast as me. Fur catches on the branches as it leaps out of danger. I fire my arrow. The creature slumps to the floor. I catch up to it and begin to stroke the soft fur. The fur begins to transform in front of me... it's not fur but hair. It's not an animal but a human... a girl... I am no longer a hunter but a killer.

Chelsea Steadman (14)
Impact Independent School, Dudley

Caught?

She was trapped and she knew it. I gripped my gun and rested it above my car door, only hearing the trembling of my hands against the door slightly. Yet, her face was still beaming. Her chase was over, didn't she know that "It's done, you've been caught!" I yelled through my riot helmet.
"Never, you'll never stop us!" her voice echoed teasingly through the open road.
"No, we-" the radio clicked.
"All units, get out here! The bridge... the bridge has caved! It's been bombed!" We turned to her as we heard her giggle. "Told you, you're too late!"

Sitara Christina Kaur Bhal (14)
Kings Monkton School, Cardiff

The Lockdown

It was free period in the library. All of a sudden, lockdown sirens whirled. My heart dropped. We scrambled under desks. *Bang! Bang!* Shots were fired. I was petrified. Shots got louder, screams got higher. The door slammed open. I told myself, *stay quiet*. But, every heartbeat was a pounding drum. Footsteps came closer, Converse high tops. I recognised him. It couldn't be. I needed a better look. No! Not him! Please, no! All I could do was freeze. He left. I shouted, "There's no need!" He pointed his gun at me. He had done it, he had found me.

Abi Thomas (13)
Kings Monkton School, Cardiff

The Golden Escape

We got out through the window into the yard. We were surrounded by guards. Rafe distracted the guards while me and Sam went through the narrow vents. "Keep going, Nate!" The dusty vents crumbled our breath. We soon got out by a watchtower and climbed it as fast as possible.
"Hola amigos!" said Rafe.
"Rafe, Nate, keep going!" Sam exclaimed. "I'll be right behind you!" We vaulted, leapt until we got to Watchtower B. Rafe and I jumped next to the watchtower. I reached out to Sam. He successfully got on as we jumped to escape jail.

Mohannad Abdulkarim Albeladi (12)
Kings Monkton School, Cardiff

They Always Run

My head aches, knees ready to collapse. My heart, equal to the thunder, thumping in the sky. My pace slackens but my fear only prospers as I hear them, getting closer. They're gaining on me. My ribs burn with every inhalation and the sweat above my lip beads in the chill of the frosty night air. I can't run for much longer, they'll catch up eventually. Perhaps they already have... perhaps they're just waiting for the perfect moment to strike. As I grow weaker, they only grow more hungry, more obsessed. I've become the prey. I've no chance. Why run?

Rachel Madeline Thomas (14)
Kings Monkton School, Cardiff

The Greatest Fear

Everything was a blur. Life flashed past me before my very eyes. Running as fast as I could, I escaped from the encasing forest. But, there was one thing I couldn't escape. Eyes. Big, gloomy, mysterious eyes coming at me from every direction. A silhouette of a figure loomed over me, coming closer and closer. Only one thought rushed through me... *Run.* I leapt over branches, trampled on the dancing grass but what I didn't know was that the worst was yet to come. I felt a cold hand crawling towards me. I turned around and saw my greatest fear...

Priyal Dilip Rupalia (12)
Kings Monkton School, Cardiff

The Hunted/Hunger Games

Pow! Ping! Slip! I was being hunted by electronic snipers. I was running at my optimum speed, trying to find any cover and gather my thoughts. Trees were a perfect place to hide. Thankfully, I was wearing camo. Bullets pinged past me. My adrenaline was pumping, my body aching. I didn't even know if I was bleeding.

Suddenly, seeing a river, I tried to scavenge for resources around my location. Like a firecracker, my brain was telling me to jump into the river and swim. As I jumped, I was flanked down the river, my heart raced... Too late...

Jacob Mankoo-Pearson (13)
Kings Monkton School, Cardiff

Hunted

The darkness was taking over. I couldn't run for much longer, he was after me. It wasn't safe. He was catching on, the demonic, ghost-like creature.
"You should give up, boy," he whispered in a deep, hollow voice.
"No!" I shouted with a panicked tone. I could hear my heartbeat pounding against my chest. I didn't know how long I could last. I was running for my life as fast as a wolf. Suddenly, I collapsed onto the ground. All I could see were the enormous trees and leaves on the ground, all lifeless. What would happen next?

Rachel Liu (11)
Kings Monkton School, Cardiff

Cub's Life

It's cold. It's the biting wind. Despite being in my natural habitat, I still lose heat so quickly. I had many joys when I was young, like the time I was fishing with my mother. Then something dark and scary made me petrify. I stood there, panicked. I was dumbstruck. My heart. She's gone. The only thing that brought me happiness, faded. I never forgave them. I knew from that day on, it's the matter of life or death. The way to freedom. They are consequences, traps, predators, hunters. I inhaled my last breath and set off to the horizon.

Johnny Jiang (12)
Kings Monkton School, Cardiff

The Poached Elephant

I can't run, my legs ache, blood dripping off them, dogs barking like savage monsters, guns firing, bullets whizzing past my face. What should I do? I have been running for hours but I could still hear dogs gnashing and gritting their teeth, hunters firing their guns with big bangs, decorating the African plains. Too tired to run, I knew I couldn't stop but I did. For five seconds there was just quiet, then dogs biting their fangs into my feet. The hunter shot. I felt the metal bullets pierce my flesh. I stumbled backwards and fell into death.

Blake Fry (11)
Kings Monkton School, Cardiff

Finding Them!

Yawn! A new day! I'll go and make breakfast! I thought. I walked happily along the landing. I went to see my mother and father first. But, they weren't there. I called for them but no reply, so I ran to Tess' room and told her. She already knew and suggested we call them. We tried but, again, no reply so we went to our brother's room and told him. He thought we should check the opera they went to last night. So we got ready and checked. Their tickets were there and said, '*We're coming for you next...*'

Hannah-Grace Hay (13)
Kings Monkton School, Cardiff

Hunted

Run. I could feel the harsh wind on my face as I leapt through the trees. Stumbling and tripping over branches, I made my way blindly through the woods. I couldn't let them catch me. Grabbing hold of the foliage in an effort to propel myself forward, my forehead beaded with sweat and my heart raced as I ran faster than I'd ever done before. But, I was running out of energy, my legs aching and my breathing was becoming shallow. I needed to rest. But, I couldn't. I couldn't stop. I had to keep going. I was almost there.

Indigo Jones (13)
Kings Monkton School, Cardiff

In Danger

I am never going to be safe again. Not while they know that I saw them. I was running frantically between the trees as if my life depended on it because it did. Something grabbed me by the ankle. I couldn't free my ankle. Then it went black. I woke up in a strange, dark room thinking this was the end.
"It's okay, I am one of you..."
All of a sudden, there was a thump on the door. "I know you're in there," a voice followed. "Open the door! Quickly, follow me!" the person who saved me said.

Amelia Jeffries (12)
Kings Monkton School, Cardiff

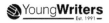

Innocent Nightmares

I couldn't do anything... I didn't want to do anything. I was branded like a cow in a slaughterhouse. Everyone knew me but not like this. You could say I have nightmares but now I'm living a nightmare. The same, awful, vivid nightmare that snakes its way into young children's minds when they're alone. I'm supposed to be the hunter. I'm scared. I could run but where to? I will *always* be found. To be alone is icy and cold, it is endless pain, an endless run, no time to stop, breathe, no time. There's really no point in running.

Ellexa Kingdon-Bevan (13)
Kings Monkton School, Cardiff

Never Mess With DNA

We were close to the exit. After two years of being trapped in the huge facility, we were near freedom (well we would still need to save the world!). All the x-creatures were chasing us. *Crash!* went the window as we broke it and jumped. We were ringing the police but running at the same time. Looking behind me, Jack got caught. "Go without me!" he yelled. We came to a dead end. A cliff. We knew it was full of chemicals. We jumped. The cops brought us home but after a while, I noticed something. I became a... pug!

Anas Mostafa Mehrez (12)
Kings Monkton School, Cardiff

The Hunted Hunter

Running swiftly, dodging all in sight, branches pushing us down as we quickly take flight. Bullets getting louder, closer in, arms reach as I soon realise I, the hunter, am being hunted. "We've almost got him!" I heard them say. Faster I ran, not taking one breath then *bang!* I see black all around. All I hear are whispers and my brother saying goodbye as he flies away into the night. I am a hunted hunter, at last, survival was the key I did not take. I will never hunt again now I'm just stuck in a cage, left to die.

Harriette Roberts (13)
Kings Monkton School, Cardiff

It's Not Mine!

I couldn't run anymore. My side was sore and I was thirsty. They all thought I stole the money but it wasn't mine. I was trying to get to the river. I hid a boat there, just in case anything like this happened. It was dark and very scary. I felt like a mouse chased by an owl. As I approached the boat, I heard something. I turned around and saw my sister. "Run!" she shouted. "The police are coming!" As I was speeding off on the boat, police cars arrived. At least I knew my sister believed me.

Lily Thomasson (11)
Kings Monkton School, Cardiff

The End!

They were there! *Nee-naw* went the sirens of Animal Patrol. Me and my family were running for our lives. "There they are, get the leopards! They'll be so expensive!" said a big, scary man with a bow and arrow. *Thwoosh!* went the arrow which had now killed my son. I was furious. I started running to him as fast as I could, feet barely touching the grounds of the wild jungle. I kept on running. I was about to get him but, suddenly, a person tapped me on the shoulder. It was a big, scary hunter with a gun.

Younis Naseem (11)
Kings Monkton School, Cardiff

The Lost Mind

It was a knock at the door, then a smash. The door opened, Chris was with his family when the clowns swarmed in. Their masks were pale white with red hair and they had dirty white shirts on. Chris turned to comfort his family to see thick red blood trickling from their gutted throats. Chris ran through the door and into the forest. His legs were giving in. He turned back, expecting to see clowns when he saw a police officer, followed by another. Then it hit him. There were no clowns. They didn't kill them. He did.

Morgan Joseph Bleasdale (12)
Kings Monkton School, Cardiff

Area 52

I didn't know where I was, all I could see was light but then these green people walked in. First thing I thought, *aliens!* But I noticed they were all panicking. I was distracted and saw the door was open. I ran like I had the Flash in me and I ran and ran. I could hear the aliens, "Noooo!" They were running after me, but I felt power... I was turning green and I could see colours no man had ever seen but then, finally, a rocket ship. I ran so fast! *Boom!* I was somewhere else. Area 52.

Ayub Khan (12)
Kings Monkton School, Cardiff

The Chase

Lonely, isolated, I'm exploring my surroundings in a field full of lush, green grass. Fading light waving across the meadow. My fleece is frosty and grubby. My ears widen. Loud, stentorian footsteps approach. I start to buck. My strong stallion legs are running as fast as the wind. I feel knife-like claws behind me. The tall, moist grass soaks my fearful body. The thumping monster got close to me. I collapse. I see it reaching over me. That last thing I felt was my body pieces leaving me. Fading away. It was over...

Molly Williamson (12)
Kings Monkton School, Cardiff

Run

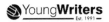

"Three, two, one, ready or not, I'm coming to find you!" I heard from Mia, the new girl who just came today. Me and the rest of the group were hiding.
I heard a voice. "No, you found me!" Me and my friend saw Mia chasing him with a knife.
My friend said, "Stop!" and Mia ran to us. We ran at super speed but Mia was the speed of lightning. Mia got my friend and she was hurting him. I kept running. I ran and ran and I never saw her again. I still have nightmares of that day!

Alexandra Marley (11)
Kings Monkton School, Cardiff

Following

I couldn't run for much longer. It was still following me. I couldn't believe this would be the end. After all I'd experienced to escape something worse than death, it was chasing me faster than ever before. My legs were going to break but I kept my determination to escape the life of the badly infected people who had the middle-man virus, a deadly virus that turned everyone one into a mutated zombie. As I ran as fast as I could, I tripped over a stone and my legs were bleeding. I fell and I was hunted.

Turki Binjubair
Kings Monkton School, Cardiff

The Pain

My legs burned, bullets inside me. Pain that I'd never felt before. I was just a boy, a boy full of dreams and a future. An ordinary Jewish boy that got his life changed. I escaped but left my family behind, behind the bars of hell. Thoughts and pain filled inside me and tears ran down my cheeks. I crawled and crawled, listening to the screams. Still, I kept on crawling until the end, the end of my dreams and future. I only had time to say my last words. They were, "The pain..." I closed my eyes...

Jerry Hongwei Liu (11)
Kings Monkton School, Cardiff

The Failed Escape!

I was sat down in a mighty bush thinking to myself whether they knew where I was. Then, suddenly, I heard a drone right above my head. I also heard someone shout, "Josh, now's your chance, get out!" So, I made a dash for it. I ran with all my strength and power until I fell, hurting myself. They made a lot of ground on me until they captured me!
They took me to court the next day and the judge proclaimed me guilty. If only they actually knew who really committed the crime. Prison conditions are so vile!

Joshua Cabaniuk (14)
Kings Monkton School, Cardiff

The Hunt

Zero, a green alien, escaped from jail without leaving a single trace. He took a motorbike and zoomed across the road. The police were right behind Zero but as the police got closer, Zero grabbed them and ate them. Zero sped up but as he did that, he puked out green goo. The police got stuck in the goo and Zero was laughing but he didn't look where he was going and *bang!* Zero hit a car and the police managed to grab him and took him back to jail.
The next day, Zero escaped again and he died.

Jacquelyn Chua (11)
Kings Monkton School, Cardiff

The Cliff

The siren wailed. They found us! We got up rapidly and started to sprint, our legs burning from escaping before we arrived in a thick forest. We were struggling to keep going, we could only see two metres ahead. We thought we had escaped them. But, it turned out they were still searching for us because we saw a searchlight heading towards us. We started sprinting, our legs started to slow down and our lungs were crying out for us to stop. But, then, we reached a cliff. We had the choice to jump or die...

Thomas Bell (14)
Kings Monkton School, Cardiff

Bad Men

I didn't know why I was running but I knew I couldn't stop. My feet were numb, my knees were aching. The stitch I had caused me agony. "Mother, I can't go on for any longer!" I cried out in pain.
"Charlie, you know we can't stop. The bad men found us! Wherever we go, it'll never be safe!" Mother trembled. I could hear the fear in her voice. I could remember the taste of ashes as they burnt down my home. I could hear the screams of the men, women and children. It was absolutely horrible.

Arjen Bhal (12)
Kings Monkton School, Cardiff

The Bomb

I had twenty-four hours to defuse the bomb, otherwise, the city would get blown up, so I ran. I ran faster than I had ever run in my life to try and get to the bomb in time but, eventually, I couldn't run for much longer. I was so close, I had to push on. Then I looked at my watch and I only had two minutes before it went off. Soon, I reached the facility and looked at my watch. I said, "I only have one more minute!" but, straight after, I saw the bomb and quickly defused it.

Jacob Thomas Chaloner (12)
Kings Monkton School, Cardiff

Hide Away

We were the last of our kind. All of them perished. We hide day and night, every breath could be our last. The men with machines that kill us all. We stay far from them. We eat very little. I reflect on the past when the days were wonderful. We hear men come, the parting screech gives me chills. We all knew that we were not going to survive. We need to march and bestow courage upon us where we can rise against them and go up against those serial killers. This would be the final battle.

Jaden Rohan (12)
Kings Monkton School, Cardiff

Fleeing The Forest

I couldn't run but was sprinting so fast after this thing. My lungs were like gunshots to the chest. As I lifted my back off the large log, a nuclear explosion roar came from the heart of the forest with leaves flying to the ground and saliva smashing the wood. As a gush of wind hit my forehead, a meteor smash came metres behind me. Turning my head to meet it, I saw no eyes, no nose when it was looking straight at me. It turned, so I threw a rock slightly to my right and it fired away.

Zachary Clarke (11)
Kings Monkton School, Cardiff

The Chase

I woke up in a cell with strong, iron bars. I heard a deep voice and a loud bark. The figure asked me my name. I replied, "Stanley."
I got up from the facility and my torso ached. The floor was made of dirt so I dug a hole. I stripped the tracker off. As I escaped the cell, I saw and smelt the local petrol station. I could not run for much longer, so I hid inside the local shops. I could feel the nice touch of snakeskin from the shopkeeper's pet. I saw my dad...

Zaid Jibril (12)
Kings Monkton School, Cardiff

Jailbreak

I was finally going to leave this place once and for all. It was going to become the past. I suddenly saw a car pass by. I had an idea. I was going to stop it. I somehow did. I climbed in and knocked out the driver. I threw him into a hedge and quickly clambered in. I could hear the cops, they had found out my location. The chase was on! I was weaving in and out, overtaking when, suddenly, a lorry pulled out. I thought we were going to crash. Suddenly, I woke up, it was a dream!

Oliver Morgan (11)
Kings Monkton School, Cardiff

On The Run!

I ran. I ran and ran as fast as my legs could take me. A man wearing a black hoodie and a mask chased me with a gun. I could hear the guns behind me. My heartbeat was so loud, I could hear it in my ears. I was walking home when, suddenly, that man pulled out his gun. He was gaining on me! I stopped in a corner, panting like a dog. There he was, walking towards me, gun in hand. Just then, the police came. Just before he stepped into the car, he shot me. Everything went black...

Manel Soleman (11)
Kings Monkton School, Cardiff

Where Can I Hide?

As I point the gun in my hand at the people at the front desk, my hands are trembling. The demand for money comes out of my mouth, as well as the intimidation from the gun, enough for them to give me money. I run out, down an alleyway. Am I safe? I think so. As I catch my breath, I see a cop in the corner of my peripheral vision. He shoots. It hits me, *bang,* in the arm. Bleeding, I run. I have found an open sewer. It's the only option. This has to be my escape.

Chris Jones (14)
Kings Monkton School, Cardiff

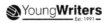

The Siren, The Wolf And The Woods

I had been running forever. The wet mud grabbed my feet. I looked up, all I could see was darkness with the bright moon creating a path amongst the trees. The trees had big, black trunks with brown, crispy leaves and they seemed to be spying on me. I heard a siren. I had to go! I ran away from it as fast as my feet would let me. Out of nowhere, a wolf jumped out at me. I fell to the floor, I felt it bite into my leg. There was no hope for me. I fell unconscious.

Lucy Robinson

Kings Monkton School, Cardiff

The Hunt

On a normal day in Wales, Bob and Tim were having a drink in a pub. Bob brought chocolate with him and Tim stole it and walked off and he never came back.
Then Bob spied on Tim to see what he was doing with it. He followed him everywhere to see if he was going to give it to anyone and he followed him in a car and train to a restaurant and so on. Bob was getting more and more angry.
On Monday, when Tim went to work in an office, there was Bob...

Oliver David Jones (13)
Kings Monkton School, Cardiff

Hunted

I couldn't run for much longer but I knew I had to keep moving. Hot on my heels was a red, furry fox. I suddenly heard a yelp from behind. I quickly turned my head and saw the fox stuck in a thorn bush, he escaped very quickly and was on my whiskers again in a matter of seconds. Ahead of me was a barbed wire fence and it had a gap in it. I managed to squeeze myself through the gap in the fence. The fox made a leap of faith at my tail. "Ow!" I screamed.

Callum Morgan (11)
Kings Monkton School, Cardiff

Midnight Feast

I ran like lightning. I had to get home before the spell was broken and the prince found I had been such a flippin' catfish. I headed towards the carriage. "Onward!" I yelled at the imaginary horses to pull me on my way home as quickly as possible. Suddenly, I heard a strike. The strike of midnight began. I felt everything around me start to change. I was sinking to the muddy depths of the woods.
As I found myself stuck in the ground, I felt something bite on my shoulder. A wolf was feasting on my life.

Lily Lorraine Rebecca Harrison (16)
Newfriars College, Bucknall

Skincrawler

There was no one in sight other than a little girl who kept turning her head and hiding behind the fences. I was so scared! I stopped. All I could see was the little girl getting closer. By the time I blinked, she was within touching distance. It then became clear that she wasn't a little girl. She was very tall. I started to run again but I knew I couldn't escape for much longer. It was still dark. I couldn't see a thing. When I turned back again, she was right there, behind me. She made my skin crawl!

Josh Taylor (17)
Newfriars College, Bucknall

Soldiers

I ran across the ground feeling frightened. I heard something trudging towards me so I looked up to see what was coming. I didn't know what it was and I wasn't sure what it looked like. It took me ages to see what the noises were and what they were doing. Then I saw soldiers. I couldn't run for much longer because I had no energy in my legs. I stood quietly and heard footsteps. Then, there were strange noises getting closer. I was so scared, I closed my eyes and waited for the end to come. All went silent.

Declan Rochelle-Peake (16)
Newfriars College, Bucknall

Stalingrad

I ran away from the soldiers of the fascist Reich. I went into an open manhole and closed it. The Germans ran past. Once I found it was safe, I climbed out and made it to the fountain. I saw two soldiers on my side and went to them. They introduced themselves as Dimitri and Viktor. Viktor asked where my squad was and I told him they'd been killed at the Stalin statue and the Germans chased me but I lost them. Viktor told me that since my commander was dead, he would lead me.

Bradley Heath (17)
Newfriars College, Bucknall

The Zombies Are Out

We are lost, free. We do not see zombies. The zombies are coming to kill the last of the people running, going into their homes. The zombies all need to kill people and make themselves a home but they want to kill more, they want to kill them all. They want to kill all the people in the world and take the world over, all in a day.

Jacob Handley (18)
Newfriars College, Bucknall

Deserter

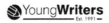

Thud. Thud. Thud. Footsteps. My footsteps. BD-021. A serial number. My serial number from the SAS. I fought in the Falklands War in the SAS as part of the BD regiment. I'd seen the atrocities of war and, well, I couldn't keep going. So, I deserted and now I'm being hunted because of it. *Thud. Thud. Thud.* Footsteps. Still my footsteps. I turn around, gasp and see my regiment's - nay, friends' - heavy-duty rifles poised to snipe me. *Thud. Thud. Thud.* My footsteps continue.
Bang! Bang! Shots fired. Then... nothing. Still nothing. Always nothing.

Thomas Griffiths (11)
Oaklands Catholic School & Sixth Form College, Waterlooville

Hunted

I couldn't run much longer. I was magical but that doesn't need a witch hunt. I was only a sorcerer's apprentice and I was about to say how we meant them no harm when they hunted me! *Crack!* A musket. They had found me. I ran for three days and I was tired. I was panting, gasping for breath. *Crack!* Hot pain seared up my chest. I looked. I'd been shot. I stifled a scream. I grabbed some dirt and threw it down. A fog arose. I cast a spell and jumped through my portal. I was safe for now...

Oliver Duffy (12)
Oaklands Catholic School & Sixth Form College, Waterlooville

Closer, Closer

I couldn't run for much longer. It was gaining on me. My heart was pounding like a drum. It was in my mouth. I was running through a tight gap. It shrank and enlarged again. My mind whirled. How could it be shrinking and enlarging again? There had to be a weak point. I hid behind a rock. The thing raced right by. Suddenly, it came to a screeching halt. It looked around, slowly. It spotted me. The chase began again, around and around the rock and then I ran off into the horizon...

Callum Anthony Vowles (13)
Oaklands Catholic School & Sixth Form College, Waterlooville

The Blazing Inferno

"We have to leave. Now!" Surprised, I turn around and stare at my mother as she hurriedly stuffs a bag with some of my clothes.

"What are you-" A whistling noise cuts me off and my mother, usually so calm and composed, frantically pulls me out of the house.

"Go, go, go!" she yells.

"What-" I'm interrupted.

"No time to explain, go!" screeches my terrified mother. And, as the sky fills with fire, I run. I run, gasping for breath. I run until I can't any more. Then the fire reaches me and I gasp my last burning, painful breath.

Fiona Manning (13)
The Matthew Arnold School, Staines Upon Thames

The Question Of Her Fate

Death. Dust. Drought. Lifeless bodies littered all over town like the streets of London. Just one was left. Locating him was hard so when we got the opportunity, we had to take it. He had killed infants, parents and grandparents. He was filth to us. So elimination was a priority. He was on top of a building with an AK-47. He was in my clear line of sight. I thought this could be over but he grabbed a three-year-old flesh shield, blocking my clear shot, putting the question in my mind, *should I or should I not?*

Jack Barber (15)
The Matthew Arnold School, Staines Upon Thames

Hell Or Heaven

I can't be in here anymore. This hell is too much for me. I imagine the life outside, beautiful, happy, nice. If only I could be there. My life would be heaven if only I could take a step outside into the world. I knew it wasn't impossible. I have tried my goal and longed for it.
I ran away from jail and saw the world. Darkness, then falls. Blue flashing lights follow me, chasing me, it's hunting me. My heart beats rapidly. I am on the run. Despair falls in my life. My life is now hell again.

Hushmeet Singh Nagpal (11)
The Matthew Arnold School, Staines Upon Thames

When Will It End?

It started when we were 16. He flipped. Changed. He was vicious, murderous, lethal. We were chased for decades and are still being hunted. There is no reason, no sanity. He has lost all sense of humanity. We may be dead soon but it was worth it. Despite being hunted for most of our lives, we got to see the world accept us, not for monsters but as people. Our father hunting us does not make us monsters, it makes us victims. My life is an endless cycle of misery. I have run for too long. When will it end?

Rebecca Steel (14)
The Matthew Arnold School, Staines Upon Thames

The Enemy Encounter

Touching down, I detached my parachute, feeling the rush of being on enemy soil. Shuddering, hearing the blast of the firearms in Asia. Few knew that there was a war happening between MI6 and MI3. In the distance, I could see the barn where I was to meet my troops. Hairs rose on my neck. I whipped around... Enemy soldiers, each holding vicious dogs and a deadly-looking rifle. I hurdled the wire fence into the shrubbery. One yelled. I scrambled, running, feet pounding, sweat dripping, branches barricading my path, heart hammering. Guards closing in. Dogs snapping. The hunt was on...

Mylea Geal (11)
The Skinners' Kent Academy, Tunbridge Wells

Hunted In War

Dear Diary,
It was horrible. I got captured by ten Germans. We were horrified every turn. Our friends killed, wounded, petrified. We ran, hid. I saw a soldier. He ran to us. Sadly, he got shot in the temple. I cried, shouting, to realise a bullet in my chest. I realised I was in hospital, seeing 200 people in one surgery. I saw blood on my chest. I yelled, "Help!"
The nurses rushed to see my mother bandaging my body saying, "How did this happen?" Then I saw my dad, sister and injured brother. They told me it was over.

Oscar Adrian Nowak (11)
The Skinners' Kent Academy, Tunbridge Wells

When Peaceful Surroundings Turned Immediately

The sun was blending into the horizon, the seawater was lashing around my body. I was lying down peacefully on my bodyboard, watching the beautiful sunset. It was midday and I was relaxing in the sea. Then my peaceful surroundings changed immediately. A dark shadow floated around the water. Then the shadow became whole. A shark was by my side. My imagination got the better of me and I swear I saw the shark licking his lips, waiting for his supper to fall into the water. Then the terrifying beast made a lunge towards his meal, which was me.

Lolita Rose Thurlwell-Stapley (12)
The Skinners' Kent Academy, Tunbridge Wells

The Dream

"We have to leave. Now," my best friend shouted in trepidation.
I looked behind us, there was a petrifying wolf chasing my friend. I had to make a distraction. While my friend was running, I stopped and picked up some filthy stones. I made a terrible choice. I threw the filthy-looking stones at the wolf. It started to chase me.
I turned around to run and my friend was nowhere to be seen. The wolf was catching up to me. My heart was racing. I was so agitated.
Suddenly, I woke up and it was all just a dream.

Ellie-Mai Glazebrook (12)
The Skinners' Kent Academy, Tunbridge Wells

The Grand Pounds

He woke, sharply stood up and ran as fast as he could. His house was a predator and he was the prey. Every night, a flush of anxiety ran over him and knocked all sense out of him, making him crazy. Flashbacks came and went but overall, all that was on his mind was the money. £2000 by tomorrow night and he hadn't got any. It made Darren do horrific things like steal and rob people of their hard-earned money. All so his selfish self could live. Sirens and lights. Noise and shouting. Bars and cells. He was caught.

Freya Myhill (11)
The Skinners' Kent Academy, Tunbridge Wells

Infected

We're not safe here, not anymore. Nowhere is safe around this place. People died trying to find a cure for this. Now, nobody is safe. It got out the lab and it's spreading all around. Soon the whole world will be infected. I run. I run as fast as I can so nobody and nothing can find me. The autumn trees swish bitter, cold air into my face. I know at once that those trees will soon be dead. I get onto the tube. I'm safe. I turn around. They're infected. So I run. I am not fast enough. Infected.

Beckett Cook (11)
The Skinners' Kent Academy, Tunbridge Wells

Race

It has to be here somewhere, we've been looking for ages. We had to find it or we would be fired. We were looking for a special cup, one that says 'The World's Best Boss'. All we could find was 'Best Dad' or 'Best Son'. We had five minutes until our boss got into work. Then I saw it. It was on a shelf by itself. I saw another group of people walking over to it, so we ran. They saw us, so they ran. It was a race. It was a race that they won, at least for now.

James Christopher Murphy (13)
The Skinners' Kent Academy, Tunbridge Wells

Hunted Down!

"I had twenty-four hours. I had to get the box, sneak past and leave unnoticed. Anyway, it wasn't even that easy. I knew I couldn't do it alone so I brought my friend, Joe, in. Unfortunately, he didn't make it though."
"Joe Williamson was it?"
"Yes, he was very secretive though!"
"Of course he was, you knucklehead, because he is working with them, you massive lump of lard!"
"Well hold on a minute, if he is working with them then we have been tracked and followed. We're about to die, aren't we? When will it be our demise?"
"Now!"

Caleb Thasan (11)
Wymondham High Academy, Wymondham

The Big One

"We have to go, they are almost here!" said Luca. The two dummies were being shot.

"Can we just get the money and go?" said Oliver.

"Get in quick, they will be here soon!" shouted the getaway driver. They were driving as the police car started rapidly shooting at them.

"Go, go!" the criminals shouted. They were almost at the meeting point. They were about to be shot as the driver was shot. Luca swiftly grabbed the wheel as the army was coming. They drove past the pick-up point and crashed into a farmer's field.

"Get down!" yelled Luca.

Harvey Norton (11)

Wymondham High Academy, Wymondham

Killer Drones Over Chernobyl

They were only worried about money, not safety. They put it to max power and then doubled it. *Bang! Bang! Bang!* The roof blew violently off, waking everybody in a ten-mile radius. They watched in desperation from Death Bridge whilst their children excitedly played in the radioactive snow that drizzled onto them. The firemen tried putting out the never-ending blaze of a nuclear core on fire.
One week later, there was a fleet of at least one-hundred planes flying over Chernobyl at once. Some killer drones were taking the planes out and on the drones, the flag read, *We're coming...*

James Philip Eddowes (12)
Wymondham High Academy, Wymondham

The Rising Dead

I only had twenty-four hours and I was on my twenty-second. Suddenly, sirens started blaring out from behind me. I ran, busting through the gates, leaving my bleeding parents stranded. I rushed into the cemetery. It was gloomy and dismal all around, shivers were creeping down my spine. As I walked along the mossy, cobblestoned path, I started to see less and less. Unexpectedly, two dark figures, side by side, emerged from the ground. It was a horrible sight. The closer they got, the more I recognised them. "Mum!" No answer. "Dad!" Still no answer. Unfortunately, they were both zombies!

Luca Beau Aldridge (11)
Wymondham High Academy, Wymondham

I'm Going Hunting

10:30. The mountain top. The rampant wind streaming through the surrounding trees. I exhale and peer through my middleman's scope. They should never forget that I always attain my shot. Your foolishness has led you to an amplified gun. The Barret 50 calibre. Steadily, I start pulling the trigger. *Bang!* I tell you, that would've given that dude one heck of a headache. What I've done, I still have nightmares. It haunts me. But, I don't regret it. Around here, it's about business. I don't want to kill by choice but every time I get richer and earn respect...

Jayden Bright (12)
Wymondham High Academy, Wymondham

Silence

A sound hammered against my eardrum. A deafening noise. Loud enough to petrify anyone who crossed it. I sat dead still behind a stack of boxes, watching my enemy's every step. I didn't dare to move in case I came face to face with death. Sweat dripped down my face as the ear-piercing screams got nearer. Helicopters flew overhead and shone streams of light onto the ground below. I looked ahead to find the police weren't there. Did they go? Could they not find me? Suddenly, a blinding light swallowed my body whole. Almost immediately, there was silence. *Bang!* Darkness.

Evie Swan (12)
Wymondham High Academy, Wymondham

Dead Or Alive

This was it, time for my escape. Me and my two friends were fed up of this asylum of Hell. 12am, everyone was asleep. It was time for action. Sirens wailed. Dogs barked. Would we make it?

"Sargeant, Prisoner 12789 is escaping, release the hounds, units in the area, now! Alert all the houses in the neighbourhood, now!"

"Run, James, run!" *Beep! Beep! Beep!*

"Hello, can you hear me?" Confused, I woke up in a daze. Where was I? Opening my eyes, all I could see was blood. Why was I handcuffed to a metal bed? I had been caught.

Harvey Crane (12)

Wymondham High Academy, Wymondham

The Midnight Horror

Lying, silence surrounding me, no movement found. Gunshots fill the air. Eerie prickles, chills flooding down my spine. Lightning strikes, thunder booms, something emerges from the corner of my room. Shadows pass my bed. All the creaking near my head. The shape of a demon, the eyes as red as the Devil's pitchfork. Then the feeling of being stalked. Out comes the knife, this could be the end of my life. I'm ending, death is closer, closer. I wish the ticking of the clock would stop, time is needed. The sharp blade hits my throat. No death. How? Sleep paralysis.

Sophie Addy (11)

Wymondham High Academy, Wymondham

We've Been Found!

We were so close but then the thing, it came out of nowhere! I had started running in the other direction, my friends either side of me. This 'adventure' had gone terribly wrong. Suddenly, someone somewhere behind me screamed. I whipped my head around and I saw them being dragged into the darkness, yelling. I realised we were picked off one by one. My beat friend running beside me collapsed, complaining that she couldn't go on. I was helping her when one of them attempted to pounce on me. She yelled, "Run!" then I sprinted further into the cave.

Georgia Farmer (12)

Wymondham High Academy, Wymondham

Stalked

I still have nightmares about it. My heart still pounds at the thought of it. Sweat drips from my head every day. This story will stop you from sleeping. Here goes nothing... My heart stopped. A strange figure was stalking me. Suddenly, it pounded at me like a cheetah hunting its prey. I sprinted into the forest. I couldn't run for much longer. "Ow!" I screamed and tripped into a ditch. The screeching sirens pierced my ears. It would never, ever find me here. I tried to get comfortable then realised it was staring over me. "Argh!" I fled...

Georgia Macduff (11)
Wymondham High Academy, Wymondham

The Knock

Today, my life transformed forever. It was a normal, sunny day and it was the weekend. I was just playing on my computer games until I heard the door slam. I realised it wasn't the wind and I knew something wasn't right. I looked outside the window and the loud, busy roads were empty. Only one strange car. I ran downstairs immediately. Everything was normal. My dad was still watching his favourite TV show. Suddenly, I heard an alarming noise, then my heart jumped into my mouth. My dad screamed, "Get under your bed, now!" Then I heard the knock...

Scarlett Derrett (12)
Wymondham High Academy, Wymondham

The Child

"Officer 856, we have some intel on the whereabouts of Mr Catch. He was last seen by satellite images on the east side of Lake Cahoon!"
"Got it," I whispered while staring at the bush ahead of me. It appeared to rustle when I looked away to answer the call. I turned on my flashlight and aimed it at the bush. The light flashed on a pale person's face with really short hair. It looked like a child but I couldn't be sure. "Hello, who are you?"
The child didn't answer. Instead, it stared at me with a nervous gaze.

Callum Bailey (13)
Wymondham High Academy, Wymondham

Bordered Freedom

It was 3am, the sirens wailed, the armoury was assaulted. Written in blood, it said, *Free us!* I saw people carrying guns and blades and guards screaming in pain from fatal wounds. The leader ordered me to open the border via the ventilation, so I did. It was suicide. I tumbled through the vents. A guard heard me so I crashed down and stabbed him in the throat. "Freeze!" Damn. It was back-up. They tackled me to the floor. Then someone grabbed me and threw a grenade.
"58371, come with me! It's me!" Freedom was awaiting me.

Ben Lehman (12)
Wymondham High Academy, Wymondham

Only 24 Hours Left

I had twenty-four hours left 'til my life would be over. I heard the sirens ringing through my ears. I couldn't run for much longer, I was running out of breath. The sirens screeched through the dark, mysterious city, helicopters flying above me, time was running out. I didn't know what to do, I couldn't do it for much longer. Then I leapt into the pitch-black alleyway. I could still see the helicopters flying over me with their huge, bright, yellow lights. I didn't know what to do, then they saw me moving. They charged with full power...

Madison Smith (13)
Wymondham High Academy, Wymondham

Volatiles

That's the eleventh police car today? I thought to myself. *Better check the radio.* The radio was dead and I could see people getting out of their cars to find out what was happening. The police had put up roadblocks and were telling people to stay in their vehicles. I was starting to worry when, all of a sudden, gunshots. I had my hands over my ears and people were out of control, running everywhere. Then, *smash!* Somebody ran into my windscreen. He was rabid and foaming at the mouth and coming towards me. The outbreak had started!

Jack Wheeler (11)
Wymondham High Academy, Wymondham

Trapped

I had twenty-four hours. Each and every time my phone went off, it felt like my heart was in the back of my throat. It made me sick to my stomach. Every single second and every single move I made was a risk. As I awakened, it was pitch-black. All of a sudden, blinding lights appeared, then I noticed everything looked the same but something was different. I rapidly tried to open the door but it wouldn't budge. "Help, please, help!" Suddenly, a blood-curdling noise started. I could hear nothing but the sirens. Viciously, the door slammed open...

Anya Dodman (12)
Wymondham High Academy, Wymondham

The Chase

Only one metre away, winding in-between the cobbled stone was thick, scarlet blood coming from an alleyway. As I turned the corner, I saw two dead, lifeless corpses in front of me. Their throats were cut, blood trickling down them. In the darkness, I saw a child, no older than seven, bawling his eyes out. "Hey, are you alright?" I called out. He came charging towards me and hugged me. Deeper in the alleyway, I could hear malicious laughing. They suddenly pounced at us with a knife in hand. "Run!" I shouted to the child. The chase was on.

Lily Sky Higgins (13)
Wymondham High Academy, Wymondham

Where Can I Hide?

Where can I hide? I heard footsteps and panicked. The police were coming. I decided to hide in my attic until they left. Hours? Seconds? I was completely unaware of time. Until, I saw the window. My only chance. Before I could jump, a loud voice called out to me. The police. "Where are you?" The attic door busted open. Panicking, I quickly leapt out of the window, landing on the wet, cold concrete. A sharp pain shot up my leg.

It was raining outside. I ran to escape when a voice shouted to me, "Don't move, or you die!"

Sophia Lam (12)
Wymondham High Academy, Wymondham

The Creature

I still have nightmares about it. It was a sunlit, Tuesday evening, (sounds delightful doesn't it?) and I was just heading home from my tiring, boring work. I was silently skipping down the long-winded highway when I heard rustling from the bush behind me. I turned around rapidly but saw nothing so I carried on, as you would. That's when I heard it again. I felt like something was hunting me down. I started striding. I could feel its breath on my neck. I awoke to the sound of something singing softly. "You're awake I see, finally..."

Lydia Phillips (11)
Wymondham High Academy, Wymondham

Messing With Mystery

"Save yourself! I'll distract, you run!" I cut my hand and left my scent there. That didn't keep him bewildered for long. I ran so fast that everything was blurry. I hindered myself, turned around to see... nothing. Then I started to swoop back. *Boom!* He was there with his blood-red eyes and thick, long teeth, just ready to take a bite. I did the first thing that came to mind and... *snap!* I broke his neck. I was mortified. I ran faster and then they all mauled me in front of my friend. Don't fight a vampire or else!

Marie Y'sanne Bari (12)
Wymondham High Academy, Wymondham

Storm Racer

Up above me, I could see it, a flashing light in the darkness. Then, suddenly, there was a voice, calling out to me but I could not be fooled. The only thing left for me to do was run. I didn't stop until I had reached the sledge. "Hike on!" I cried and we sped away into the night. Faster and faster we went, across ice and snow until we came to a cave. "They'll never find us here" I shouted. But, before we could hide, we were surrounded. "Attack!" I commanded, sprinting forward with my axe. "This ends now!"

Kate Groom (12)

Wymondham High Academy, Wymondham

Area 51's Unknown Secrets

I knew it wasn't safe here. It had been twenty-four hours since the raid. There were hazards all around. Aliens everywhere with their green flesh and eyes like night. They tormented everyone in reach, killing thousands. I was petrified. I had been hiding in this dark laboratory by myself for a day now and I was frightened they would find me. I was starting to become famished and parched and willing to venture out when suddenly, I looked into the gloom of the dusky shadows across the room and heard an almighty crash and I realised I wasn't alone.

Lola Fortescue (13)
Wymondham High Academy, Wymondham

Death

I can hear them. I know they're coming. Hunted! A pack of foul, evil, loathsome creature that by day lurk in the shadows and by night suck your blood. "Ow!" The pain, not from my mangled leg, courtesy of my evil friends, but my heart throbbing with heat. I can't move, they're getting closer. My breath is depleting. In the last moments of my life, I decide to have courage. People have died for me, us. All those people uninjured and dauntless because of me. I can't stand it! This will end now, one more life will be taken tonight.

Camille Wright
Wymondham High Academy, Wymondham

The Victoria Square

I was bursting, cars whizzing past me... unless... Victoria Square had a toilet! But, there was a twist. It was 200 years old. I would be wise not to go in. I had no choice. It had been blocked before since people had gone missing but I didn't think twice. Frantically, I dashed down the tunnel and opened the door. Then, a crash like a rusted door being slammed. "It's just the wind..." I said to my extremely tense self. Then, tapping. The sharpening of a kitchen knife. A deafening laugh that faded into footsteps. Footsteps towards me...

Leon Etynkowski (12)
Wymondham High Academy, Wymondham

The Hunt

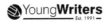

They were closing in on us, we didn't have much time. A broken gas pipe hissed as we hurtled past, giving off a foul stench. We sprinted through the city centre as crowds of terrified people parted before us. Gunshots fired and sirens wailed. Behind us, people dropped to the ground, shot dead. Now everyone was trying to escape, the few that survived the shooting limped and stumbled. We backed into an alley by a main road. Bombs were dropped. The silhouette of our vicious hunters danced on the surrounding floor and walls. We tried to run. A dead end...

Chloe Barr (11)

Wymondham High Academy, Wymondham

Trade Item

Apparently it's a good thing, the way I'm in demand like a trade item. I am aware that my intellectual ability is higher than average but does everyone need to know? Even my parents have been brainwashed by the reporters, ferrying me to speeches and presentations. They aren't the only people; friends use me to cheat during tests and our principal sees me as an empty chequebook with the pages safely in his pocket. Not only am I hunting for an exit from this spotlight but I'm also being hunted by the very people I thought I could trust.

Katie Smith (13)
Wymondham High Academy, Wymondham

I Am Hunted

I'm Elanor. I've been hiding from the Coggs-Mission for months. I know that I'm not safe now that they know what I am... an elemental. I bear something they want, the fire elemental crystal my mother gave me before she was killed. Now, I'm officially on the Coggs-Mission hunted list, only allowed to place my trust in a handful of people. At least I have Spock, my faithful mechanimal who hasn't left my side. But now I'm running for my life, never knowing what will happen next. So, this is a life on the edge, running, running...

Ella Harrison (11)

Wymondham High Academy, Wymondham

That Night

We knew this idea was stupid but we thought it was funny at the time. My friend, Sarah, went one route and I diverted the other. We had our phones switched on in case we needed each other.
The night was getting lightless and the trees were creaking. I thought to myself, *something is out there.* All of a sudden, I came across a creepy, primitive wooden cabin. As I took one step forward I discovered a deafening scream from inside and a penetrating blade blinded me through the window. I sprinted away. Then a black figure pounced before me!

Tallie Chilleystone (12)
Wymondham High Academy, Wymondham

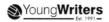

Running Against The Clock

My hand was firmly pressed up against my chest, the pressure slightly numbing the throbbing pains. I was covered in blood but I couldn't stop running now. I'd been doing this for too long to surrender. The border was vaguely visible, yet it was easy to spot the monstrous swarm of helicopters and drones above me, stalking me, watching, filming, tracking my every move. They were sinister and as black as a storm. I was close but nowhere near close enough as the dark blood fell down and my body began to ache even more. I tried to keep running...

Ellis Ivany (11)

Wymondham High Academy, Wymondham

The Hunt Was On

I couldn't run for much longer. My legs were slowing down. The pain was unbearable. I could stop running but they wouldn't stop searching. I was able to hear the wailing of sirens and the propellers whipping round and round. I was waiting for the end of the noise however, that moment would not come. My legs were burning and my torso ached. Every breath was like someone stabbing me in the throat. My adrenaline rushed. I scanned the area and a cliff edge was crumbling. Flashing lights surrounded me. I looked for another exit. That was the only way.

Hattie Finch (11)
Wymondham High Academy, Wymondham

Running

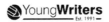

Sirens burned through the night. Blood dropping through the lethal forest. Time was running out. Running, I couldn't run for much longer. As I held on to my life, I knew I wasn't safe and I never would be, so I knew I had to go. Gluey purple blood stuck to every spiky tree I passed. It was the only weapon I had against those people, screaming, shouting, "Help!" Ships landed everywhere, there was nowhere to go. I hid in the undergrowth like everyone else. They grabbed people out... Suddenly, I was in sitting in my room on my bed.

Beth Lawrence (11)
Wymondham High Academy, Wymondham

On The Run

Climbing further up the treacherous, steep mountain, screeching filled the air, their bloodthirsty teeth ground together as we both chased for the location. The air began to get thinner. I paused, gasping for breath. They scratched at the ground as they continued to pursue me, my legs trembled on the rock. Soon enough they started to catch up, they came into view, their limbs dangled, their flesh mauled. I tried to keep up my pace but my legs told me no. I decided to hide, hoping they didn't find me, hoping I wouldn't be eaten alive...

William Pratt (13)
Wymondham High Academy, Wymondham

The Escaped

My heart was racing as I looked for my friend who'd escaped with me. My throat was hoarse with fear, every breath felt like pins in my lungs. Through the forest I raced, trying to ignore my arm, bleeding after ripping out my facility tracker. The minute I fled, I'd heard gunshots from behind and I looked back, catching a glimpse of lights from torches. I stumbled over a body, my friend who had been shot in the leg. "8264935, wake up!" I shook him gently, then vigorously. He would not awaken and green blood trickled, bubbling from his wound...

Pippa Fincham-Hawkes (11)

Wymondham High Academy, Wymondham

Hunt And Seek

Where can I hide? Everyone panicked to find the perfect place. It was shadowy, the only glow coming from an eerie house. *But, who would live in the middle of a nightmare?* I wondered. I was no longer in the forest. I was lost! I still have nightmares about it. I cluelessly walked for hours. I realised I wasn't alone. What was it? I was petrified. I could hear my heart in my ears. That melancholic feeling stalking me. I screamed for help but nobody heard. It got closer. Surely someone would wonder where I was? Then I saw it...

Chloe Russell (12)
Wymondham High Academy, Wymondham

Maya's Birthday

Molly only had fifteen minutes left until Maya's birthday party and she had to buy her best friend's dress, present and birthday cake! Maya's mum expected a lot from everyone, especially Molly as she had such an important job. It took at least ten minutes to get to the city and Molly's mum's car had stopped working. It was a long walk to the bus stop. By the time they got to the end of the road, the bus door was shutting. They both ran for their lives. This was the only bus for half an hour. They just couldn't wait...

Anna Pond (12)
Wymondham High Academy, Wymondham

Silhouette

It was a dark, gloomy night. I couldn't move a muscle. I was terrified. In the corner of my eye, I spotted a shadowy silhouette. I was wondering what it was. Could it be from another planet? Another universe? Suddenly, it took one monstrous step forward but it was still just in my line of sight thought. Unexpectedly, the figure vanished. In the blink of an eye, it emerged, now close enough to give me instructions from afar. All of a sudden, I spotted a glimmering knife clutched in its hand. We were in touching distance and... I woke up.

Freddie Folkard (11)
Wymondham High Academy, Wymondham

Shadow Brick Wall

Running down the hill as quick as possible, I chased the black figure, trying to catch whatever 'it' was.
Earlier that night, a house got burgled. The police arrived shortly after, finding a body. No one knew who it was that had died. I was quietly asleep when the police siren woke me up. I joined everyone outside; suddenly, a shadow sped past me from behind a bush. I pursued it down the hill. I slowed to catch my breath, watching the figure get smaller. It turned round to look at me, then he faceplanted into a brick wall...

Tilly Matthews (11)
Wymondham High Academy, Wymondham

Refuge

They had broken us; they found me trying to cross the border. I didn't have much time. I just couldn't go to Sovegarde just yet. The imperials had us tied up with thick ropes. I wasn't going to let that stop me. I waited for my chance and I leapt out of the carnage, stumbling over. It didn't take long for them to realise. The chase was on... I panicked as arrows flew past my head shouting, "Get that pesky Nord!" I tripped over a branch and decided to stay there, waiting for the voices to stop. Divines, help me.

Kylar Cooper (12)
Wymondham High Academy, Wymondham

Caught

I entered the bedroom. There it was. I stuffed it into my bag and made to leave. *Creak!* I froze, my skin turning to ice. I darted my eyes, searching for danger. I saw it, two luminous eyes staring at me. It stepped forward, a man materialising out of the shadows. As he advanced, I stumbled backwards and fell. Fear engulfed me. I leapt to my feet, adrenaline forcing me to run, clouding my mind. I made for the door but there was another giant-man. He knocked me to the floor, raised his gun and fired a single shot. *Bang!*

Freddie Gent (11)
Wymondham High Academy, Wymondham

Prison Break

The sirens started whining faintly in the deep, dark, cold distance. From experience, I'd only have three hours to get away before they got to me. I'd tried to escape a few times before but the feds always found me. But, this time, I tried a different route and it was working. The sirens were slowly getting louder. I ran through small, dark alleyways. Each puddle I stepped in made my feet wetter and colder. It felt like I was running on glass. As I ran further, not knowing where I was, I could hear the sirens getting closer...

Alfie Holmes (12)
Wymondham High Academy, Wymondham

Hunted

Water swirled around me, trapping me in a torrential prison. I could feel them advancing on me. The shore wasn't far but every flail of my legs convulsed my body more than the last.
My limp body floats on the water, rocking to and fro on the waves.
No. I didn't just see that. That was not my future.
I threw my chest at the waves, breaking through them and catching a glimpse of my target. Dry land. But I was too late. I felt a freezing hand clasp itself around my ankle and I knew I'd seen my future.

Douglas Aitchison (12)
Wymondham High Academy, Wymondham

The Heirloom

Aches that I've never had before took over my body. I couldn't run much longer. My heart dropped as I couldn't find it. I stopped under what looked like shelter. Little did I know what was coming my way next. I panicked as I saw headlights crawl around the corner as if they were looking just for me. A growing conversation echoed into my ears, then I realised it was Diablo. He was furious. He knew I had it and where I was. Suddenly, the conversation stopped. I shuddered as I heard the click of a gun. "Come out!"

Fiona Eze
Wymondham High Academy, Wymondham

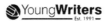

The Collapsing

The sun was radiant on a California day and news that the Earth was collapsing spread like a wildfire. We were told that we had one hour until it got to California. When the news got back to me, I packed my stuff and hopped in the car and headed towards the airport. This took thirty minutes. I booked a flight and was ready to leave. but then I saw things falling in the background. It got closer. Noise of people screaming amplified. The plane started to take off. We reached the height limit. Then the engine stopped. We descended...

Declan Magin (12)
Wymondham High Academy, Wymondham

Spiders

The bodies hung, coated in the thick, sticky web. Spiders were nowhere to be seen. That's because I cannot see through walls. I can feel their thin legs, all eight of them, every time I touch the hollow walls of this house. Why am I in this house? Because I am not out. Why am I not out? Because I cannot get out. Why can I not get out? Because someone locked me in here. Someone put these spiders in here. Someone that let these people become spider corpses. Victims of the grotesque beings crawling towards me right this second...

Olive Christien-Relph (12)
Wymondham High Academy, Wymondham

Zombie Escape

I see someone and, being a zombie, I chase after him. I run and run and run but despite my best efforts, he gets away. The dark sky of a nuclear winter loomed over the whole world. Most people are dead or infected but the uninfected, called Anti-zoms, are easy targets. I see a lone Anti-zom so I run, charge and race towards them. They have no chance. I lunge forward and try eating his brain. Unfortunately, three Anti-zoms rush to save the loner and I flee, knowing I would have been shot otherwise. But I will rise again. Hahaha!

Sam Heaton (12)
Wymondham High Academy, Wymondham

Nowhere Is Safe!

The sirens wail in my ears, we have to leave. We're on the move again, nowhere is safe. Bright stars shine on me. I am a state, straggly, scruffy hair, my T-shirt ripped, bloody wounds. But, I don't care, I can't. I don't have time. Gunshots echo around me. I grab Alex. "We have to go!" We sprint down the alley. I keep asking myself, is it all my fault? I realized I am in a world of deep thoughts. *Bang!* My thoughts fade. I collapse and fall to the ground, bawling blood. I'm dead... or am I?

Sky Manning (11)

Wymondham High Academy, Wymondham

My Mind's Maze

I'm stumbling through an endless labyrinth through my mind. There's no escape. Every decision I make is a new twist or turn. I only seem to be making the wrong ones. Every decision I make will change me for better or worse. I can't pick the right way for everyone. No matter what, it's always incorrect. Every turn I take, I end up with another wall to scale. I'm trapped in my own mind, the taunting, twisted place that it is. Alone. I am both the hunter and the hunted, playing a life-long charade with myself, losing every round.

Emily Morton-Standley (13)
Wymondham High Academy, Wymondham

Death Day

Death reeked out through the land as I realised everyone was dead. But I stayed alive, following my own rules. First rule, stay away from crowded places. Stay curious, don't be a hero. They were the main ones as the zombies hunted me. After someone was infected, the fat people died first. As I was chased through the woods by the psychos trying to eat me, the zombies screeched, attracting more. I knew I was gonna trip. There I went, faceplanting the ground. I shot one then I ran away to safety in a car. Then I started to drive.

Adam White (12)
Wymondham High Academy, Wymondham

The Chase

The sirens wailed. I could feel the pricks from all of the bushes and the stings, the bee stings that kept coming back. That feeling, that pain! The police chased me, the lights, the sounds, the pain. "Stop right there!" It's because of all those people. All the signs, now the police are after me. I jumped the prison wall. I knew I shouldn't have done it. One of them shouted, "I see him!" He was getting closer and closer. I came to a dead end. I gave up. It was my time, my time to go back to prison.

Oliver Edward Prior (11)
Wymondham High Academy, Wymondham

The Haunted Hunter

My last chance to live... it all started when I went for a picnic with my family in the woods. I got lost, separated from them, wandering further and further into the dark wood. I felt a cold breath trickling down my spine. Turning briefly, all I could see was darkness. My heart skipped a beat. I could hear the crashing of a tree. An icy-cold figure touched my shoulder. The voice of a ghost ripped through my spine. "Turn back..." I hastily ran, not stopping, tripping up as I went. I felt something behind me, then darkness...

Olivia Bullen (12)
Wymondham High Academy, Wymondham

Zombie Invasion

I sprinted as fast as I could and front flipped over a wall that was in my way. I chucked a grenade into a building and killed a big horde of zombies. I had to catch the devilish doctor that created these monsters. I heard machine guns fire and cars blowing up. The doctor stumbled into a dead end. *Finally*, it was my chance! Suddenly, zombies came pouring in. I took out my mini-gun and obliterated all the zombies. I got my pistol and aimed it at the doctor's head. I was ready to pull the trigger. *Bang!*

Oscar Woods (11)
Wymondham High Academy, Wymondham

The Chase

I woke up to sirens wailing and people shouting. But, I worried because I couldn't find anybody in the house. I couldn't find my mum, dad, brother, sister or dog. Nobody. I was panicking, so I raced outside to look for them. I ran for miles, thinking I was a super-fast runner but as I passed the bushes, they looked like they were moving as slow as snails. I was losing my strength but I needed to find them. "They have to be here somewhere!" I said. But I didn't know where. Sirens, shouting, screaming, darkness, no one near.

Katie Woodcock (11)
Wymondham High Academy, Wymondham

The Last Breath

I didn't dare look back. I needed to get off the streets and somewhere safe. The forest, that was my only hope. My pace was slowing but I urged myself to carry on. My amber eyes flickered from left to right, scanning the streets for people. I reached the forest. I could hear my every, heavy breath like a drum. I felt the blood running through my veins. I was uncontrollable. Some would say I was wolf-like. I could hear them now. I began to hallucinate. I was in their sights. I took what I thought was my last breath...

Tabitha Hearn (11)
Wymondham High Academy, Wymondham

Confusion

As I was on my daily run, I saw something in the trees across the road from me. It passed through my mind, I didn't think anything of it.
It started to play on my mind as I approached my house. I unlocked the door and strolled in. I bolted it behind me. Seconds later, the door crept open. The air was still. My mind was baffled. "I thought I had locked the door!"
I walked over to the entrance, processing my every move. I got over to the door, slammed it shut. Milliseconds later, I heard a noise...

Cullum Harvey (12)
Wymondham High Academy, Wymondham

Scientific Robbery

A piercing howl filled the sky. I stopped in my tracks, panting in fear. I ran past the gnarled tree trunks with the thorns nipping at my heels. It is the year 2039 and life is very different now. The land is roamed by strange things all because of a scientific robbery.
A few years ago, a scientist made a formula that made you into anything you wanted. Someone assassinated the scientist and stole the formula. The world turned chaotic and no one could stop it. My parents got caught up in. I was left alone one day...

Shamiso Amanda Mutokonya (11)
Wymondham High Academy, Wymondham

The Day My Dog Went Berserk

I still have nightmares about this one man. He was no ordinary human. If you even stepped onto his premises, you would be hunted. His hands were claws and he was as fast as a cheetah. He had a black ponytail hanging out the back of his silky, black mask. I never thought of even seeing him. He was based in an abandoned forest. He would only appear on a misty night.

Once, I went to walk my dog through this dark, gloomy habitat, keeping my guard. But, my dog started going berserk and I heard a high-pitched screech...

Marcus Dunn (12)
Wymondham High Academy, Wymondham

Who Rules The World?

Every step felt like being stabbed in the leg. I could hear the cracks and bangs followed by screams. The infinite amount of tree stumps were passing me as I ran past the final signs of plant life. Right now, it is the year 2350 and AIs have taken over the world. They believe that life is pointless and have killed all life in the world. I hid behind a pile of bricks which may have once been a house. I heard the robotic voices getting closer. My heartbeat quickened and metallic faces stared from above. Another casualty.

Ethan Tomkins

Wymondham High Academy, Wymondham

The Dark Room

I sat there, giving my target the death stare. He was chatting to his mates. Suddenly, he stopped talking and looked at me. I looked away. He came charging down the hall with his bloody knife in his hands. I didn't realise he was coming towards me. I ran down the hall too. I hit my knee on the corner of the chair. I fell over into this room, it was dark and gloomy. I could hear him getting closer. I shuffled my way to the corner and sat there in silence. But, suddenly, the door creaked open. "Help me..."

Isla Trinity Hurrell (11)
Wymondham High Academy, Wymondham

Blue Lights

The sirens wailed as I threw the cash in the getaway car. A bright light from a helicopter formed a circle around us, telling everyone we were doing something bad. I drove at great speed, seventy, eighty, ninety, one-hundred. The car hit a curb that flipped it on its roof. I ran faster than I ever had before. I ran down winding roads and scaled up walls. I couldn't run much further. I turned the final corner to the safe house. I ran even harder when I heard a helicopter followed by a screech of sirens. I was trapped.

Jacob Dyer (12)
Wymondham High Academy, Wymondham

Hunted By My Mind

I had changed. There was no turning back now. A cold, icy hand rested on my bare, exposed shoulder. How long had I been running for? Three minutes? A chill ran down my spine. I whirled around, not willing to go down without a fight. My heart skipped a beat. He was there! I bolted for it, my leg dragging behind me and my feet stinging as they slammed down on the tarmac. I was in agony. There was a horrifically blinding white light clouding my vision and blotting out the twilight night sky. He phased in front of me...

Benjamin Miles (11)
Wymondham High Academy, Wymondham

True Horror

I woke up in a jungle. Suddenly, I stood up with speed. I heard clicking, it was coming from the trees. I didn't think much of it, so I started walking to find water. I didn't find any so I built a shelter and, out of nowhere, I heard footsteps and that clicking. When I went to look, there was a strange creature, all black. It was horrifying, no eyes, no face, just a big mouth. It saw me somehow. It screeched. It was ear-piercing. I started running. I could hear that thing behind me and then, agonising pain.

Cooper Lecaille
Wymondham High Academy, Wymondham

The Great Exhibition

The sirens wailed on the night of my fourteenth birthday. I never forgot that night and I never will. I must get revenge. Twelve years later, I trained for the army and I was to go to the greatest exhibition of my life. I would finally get revenge. I sat in a small room while the leader explained what I would do. I would wait downtown until the deafening sirens rang and then... war!

The day had come and the sirens screeched. I was ready! Ready as anything. At the time, I was hunting but soon I was hunted.

Eden Dennis (12)

Wymondham High Academy, Wymondham

Running Away

We were close but yet so far. Time wasn't on our side and it was fading away quickly. I couldn't run for much longer, my legs were tired. They felt like wobbly jelly on a plate. As my pace gradually began to decrease. I heard the vague ringing of sirens. They were edging ever-closer to me. My time was up. The sirens were louder than I had ever heard before. I caught a glimpse of a police car! I dove into a nearby bush. Waiting, my heart pounded out of my chest. I was completely surrounded. This was the end.

William Percival
Wymondham High Academy, Wymondham

The Escape!

I need to escape. Now. They're after me, with weapons. If they catch me, they'll kill me. I wasn't even there when it happened! They still think it's me, even my family are suspicious. I can't focus on how to escape with all this running through my mind. All I need to think is *run*... I pack as quickly as I can but it isn't fast enough. Had I wasted too much time thinking? They are ready to break down my door. I need to leave another way. They have completely surrounded my house. I am trapped. All alone...

Erin McGrotty (12)
Wymondham High Academy, Wymondham

Run

We had to leave. Now. We had no choice. They had parked their car outside. I could see it. I saw him take one step out of the car and he scanned his surroundings. I ducked. He looked my way. I could see their yellow torches bearing in the distance. We were going to get found. We needed to leave! I started running with my inmate struggling behind, trying to make plans if we got caught. Again. We sprinted across a busy road and jumped in a nearby ditch. Although it was ridiculously muddy and wet, we had no choice.

Carly Jermyn (12)
Wymondham High Academy, Wymondham

My Worst Nightmare

I was terrified. I saw some frightening masks gaze through the steamy window. I heard a deafening bang at the door. *Bang! Bang! Bang!* They said it was the delivery man. I had a roommate at the time. I remembered he went out for tea. I went to look through the window but that would be too obvious so I went to the peephole. Someone had started to kick the door down. Then out the window was a white van with masked people around it. Suddenly, the door slammed on the floor. It was the worst day of my life.

Riley Patrick (12)
Wymondham High Academy, Wymondham

Into The Night

The knife entered the man's chest as quickly as it had left. He slid the dagger back into the case embedded in his arm. The boy panicked. How hadn't he thought of it? The stupid implants in his eyes! Moments later, he heard the sirens wailing. Not even the bright neon lights of the city could drown out the distant, flashing lights of the police. He heard the car pull up behind him. The boy tilted his head so he could just see the police out of the corner of his eye. "Stop!" but the boy slipped into the night.

Ollie Rowe (12)
Wymondham High Academy, Wymondham

The Last Secret

They knew. They knew what I had done and I didn't know how to fix it. It wasn't safe for me to be here anymore. Abominable events of last night replayed in my head over and over again. I had to leave and fast. The final secret was out and everyone hated me for it. I wished I could just disappear. Run away and never return. I could never forgive myself for what I had done. I had twenty-four hours left on this planet and they were coming too slow. The search had begun. They were coming for me. Hunting.

Zoya Bokhari (12)
Wymondham High Academy, Wymondham

I Am Hunter

I could see them but if they could see me, I had no idea. My army had their guns pointed and they were ready to hunt. "It's not safe now they know," he whispered in my ear, his voice mysterious and his face unknown. That night, my father told me to run and never look back. My knees buckled and I fell to the ground. This was the first time I had looked back in twenty years to those days. The days when I wasn't the hunter but the hunted. Screams filled the air from those being hunted by me...

Phoebe Blake (12)

Wymondham High Academy, Wymondham

Police Chase

This was my last chance to escape. The police had been chasing me down for hours. I outran them and hid behind a bin. I stood, crouched behind the bin waiting for them to leave the area. I tried not to breathe heavily to give my position away. One of the police shone a beaming light at me. He shouted, "It's all clear. He's not here!" I thought he had found me. my heart was pounding out of my chest. I peeked my head out to see if it was all clear. "I have found him! Get him, now!"

Joel Blackburn (13)
Wymondham High Academy, Wymondham

Hunted At Dawn - Diary Of An Elephant

May, Thursday 12th, 2008.
Dear Papa, I wish you were still here. Me and Mummy are the only ones left.

May, Friday 13th, 2008.
Dear Papa, as the sun rose, we had to go into hiding. I heard the approach of the shootings. I sprinted towards Mummy, my heart was pounding. Soon enough, I pounced on her. She was still asleep. It was too late. The men were lifting her into the van, taking her away. She was dead, all my family! Now, it's my turn to face them. It's my turn to get hunted...

Janka Lisa Tuma (12)
Wymondham High Academy, Wymondham

The Hunter Who Hunted

I looked through the scope and had the perfect shot on him and was about to squeeze the trigger. He'd be dead for sure but I was pulled back and everything went black. As I was squinting, sirens blared and gunshots were fired. Then the man stood over me and I vaguely saw him pull out a gun. So, I used my quick wit and kicked up and fell off a four-storey building and then... *splat!* He was dead; he wasn't even twitching. When I turned around, the only thing I thought was, I was a hunter who hunted.

Robbie Huson (12)
Wymondham High Academy, Wymondham

The Ring Holders

I'm still haunted by it. I was the rabbit and they were the fox. They had me tied up around their fingers. I heard a gunshot and my heart stopped. I stood in silence as blood started gushing out of my side and every breath I took felt like someone was jabbing me. Sirens screeched and my head spun like a spinning top. I ran, getting further away with every step I took. It was my natural instinct to run when I was in danger. Now, it is my personal mission to get revenge and kill the unmerciful Ring Holders.

Emily Norton (12)
Wymondham High Academy, Wymondham

The Secret

I have to leave. He wants me... he wants me dead. It doesn't matter that we are related because... I know his secret. He needs me dead. After all, he couldn't let his secret get out. I am running from my dad, he will kill me if he finds me. After all, he killed his wife, his son, even his own mother and hundreds of unsuspecting children. My father is a murderer. That secret could bring him a lifetime in prison or worse, his death. I can hear him, he is coming. He's seen me... "Argh!"

Holly Gadsby
Wymondham High Academy, Wymondham

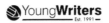

Escape: Failed

We were close but now I see we would never have been able to escape. I would probably be trapped with my dog for the rest of my life. It was not safe for me or my family now they knew what we were. A firm grip appeared on my shoulder, tightening, squeezing, forcing me forward. I struggled for breath. My dog seemed to be in the same pain as me. Cracking sounds projected from my shoulder. Screaming in pain, I shoved them back, scrambling to my feet. Making a run for the door, I heard a gunshot. Darkness...

Mia Croft (12)

Wymondham High Academy, Wymondham

The Chase

I heard the wailing sirens in the distance. They were coming! My heart was pounding and aching inside my chest. I climbed out of the ditch and ran as fast as my legs could carry me. *Bang!* Darkness. I began to see light again. Blue and red lights were now the only lights in sight. They had caught me! I was in cuffs. They shoved me in the car and took me away. My life was about to end. But, wait. It wasn't a real cop. I recognised him. No, it couldn't be... why? Why me? My end is coming...

Layla Hart
Wymondham High Academy, Wymondham

The Hunt

My heart was beating at the speed of light. The sirens wailed and the chase was on. I had twenty-four hours to run as far as possible or else... I was dead. I blindly sprinted down the dark, silenced alleyway. I couldn't see a thing as I tripped over a rock. My face drained in colour as footsteps crept towards me. I was now shaking as my veins had turned into nerves and my heart was beating faster than ever. I turned around to see my neighbour's cat emerging from the shadows. As I got up, he was there...

Evan Day (12)
Wymondham High Academy, Wymondham

The Run Away

I couldn't run for much longer, he was running after me. Ow! I fell to the ground, all I could see were trees around me. I tried to get up but I just couldn't, it was like someone was holding me to the floor. I suddenly heard a whisper sound behind me. I tried to turn my head but I couldn't. I wanted to know what was bothering me. I didn't know what to do, I was possessed. Out of nowhere, my eyes started to get extremely hot. *Poof!* I could not see anymore. Who was this creature?

Rhys Henry (12)
Wymondham High Academy, Wymondham

The Escape

Finally, I escaped the disgusting prison but what should I do now? I haven't been set free for at least forty years. The first thing I do is run for a life or death situation. Then a deafening siren raised to my ears. Blue, flashing lights in the corner of my eye. I ran like a lightning bolt shooting across the sky, my heart wanting to run but I suddenly froze and obeyed what was said. That was my only chance and I blew it. I set foot into this prison. Will I ever escape this disgusting, smelly prison?

Leah Davis (12)
Wymondham High Academy, Wymondham

Mystery Murderer

It was around two years ago. I lived in a bungalow. I was watching TV when my parents left for a party. So, when they had left, I noticed a figure in the picture frame. it was a killer from TV. I was terrified. After five seconds, I walked into the kitchen. I called the police, then grabbed a knife. I went out the back door. I started climbing the fence when the man grabbed my leg. Then I threw the knife at his leg. I ran to the front. The police had arrived. They checked the back. He'd disappeared.

Charlie Browning (13)
Wymondham High Academy, Wymondham

Hunted

I am running through a deep, dark forest. It is pitch-black. I can hear the howling of the wolves. I am being hunted. I can't escape. I am hopeless. I want to be free. I can't run for much longer. Their pattering paws get louder and louder. They are getting closer and closer. Then... it goes silent. I can't move or speak. I am frozen to the spot. Lights appear. I am blinded. I feel dead and lifeless. I drop to the floor, motionless, left here to be devoured by the wolves. I hear voices. Is it too late?

Jack Prentice (12)
Wymondham High Academy, Wymondham

The Target

I froze and, like a statue, edged towards the target. He would feel my rounds again. Inches an hour, I craned my neck, checking my flank. My goggles were running out. I had to hurry up. I was closer now but the sun was coming up. As he came out for a cigarette, I breathing out, zeroing in on his head and *boom!* I high-fived myself as his head splattered up the wall. I was done and I would see them again. Not restrained or held hostage, but free. I slumped forward. As I did, the sirens howled...

Daniel Arthur Ecclestone (12)
Wymondham High Academy, Wymondham

Running From Crisis

All he knew was that he was being hunted. A shadow had been following him for months. He hadn't realised until two days ago when he was lying, bored, in his bed but that didn't matter now. All that mattered was escaping. He couldn't live with what he had done but he had to believe he was doing the right thing. The ship was miles away and the shadowed being was getting closer. If he had never done what he did, none of it would have happened. But, he had and the whole world was suffering because of it.

Jack Sturman (12)
Wymondham High Academy, Wymondham

The Hitman's Story

I was a hitman before I was bunked up in prison. Ah, the good old days. I killed around fifty men, never women or children. I only killed the people that owed me money. One day, I anxiously sat waiting for my target, the mayor. You see, the mayor was not a delightful man. In fact, he abused his wife and kids. As the generous man that I am, I did them both a favour and fired two gunshots into his head. Anyway, let's not celebrate my awesomeness. Where are my manners? Who are you, my darling child?

Cerys Emeerith-Burley (13)
Wymondham High Academy, Wymondham

The Escape Room!

I had ten hours to escape. My heart was pounding and my throat was dry. Everyone else had left, leaving me to find it on my own. I looked around. There were multiple doors and, somewhere, multiple keys. Where were they? I found a key. I didn't know if it was right. My legs started shaking whilst I slowly twisted the doorknob. The door opened, however, I heard the *tick-tock* of the bomb. It was the wrong door. I had been hit, badly hit. I had a dark purple bruise on my temple. My time to go...

Rosie Langley (13)
Wymondham High Academy, Wymondham

The Infected

It was the year, the day. The apocalypse was here. A virus escaped from a laboratory and was infecting people faster than any disease before. Today is the day I turn from the hunter to the hunter. I knew I had to head North but I'd already not stopped in a week. I had to keep moving because if I stopped, I was dead. I knew the further North I went, the infected couldn't follow and would freeze with the wild animals ready to attack. I had to keep moving and I knew that the infected were close already.

Joseph Milburn (12)
Wymondham High Academy, Wymondham

The Chase

I could hear the engines revving. It was now or never. I had got to do this. I desperately didn't want to. What was happening to me? I hated it. As the rain started to come down, I knew it was going to get stronger. Flashing lights everywhere, gunshot bangs getting closer. My ears rang. I had to go. Did I want to die today? Give up? What did I do? I really hoped my family were on the other side like they promised. I heard burning screams. I had got to do this now. I had to jump! *Splash!*

Maisie King (11)
Wymondham High Academy, Wymondham

The Shadow

I heard footsteps. I had no choice but to run. The footsteps became louder and louder. Someone was behind me. There was no other option so I started to sprint through the dark forest with tall trees towering upon me. In the distance, I saw my escape but I didn't know if I would even make it there. When I turned around, I saw nothing but yet still heard footsteps slowly creeping towards me. Suddenly, I saw a shadow. I was so close to my escape. I thought I was going to take my very last breath...

Georgia Owen (12)
Wymondham High Academy, Wymondham

The Predators

Revenge was what I was set on with rage from watching my family get slaughtered before my eyes. Now I'm committed to murder their killer. There was no time, I had to go so I drew my gun from its holster and slowly made my way to the bunker. Unfortunately, there was a huge turret with loads of guards and armed soldiers. An SMG couldn't take on all of these soldiers, even if I had two more people with me, I could never beat them. But, if I turned back now, I would also fail. So, I stupidly attacked...

Rory Stevens (11)
Wymondham High Academy, Wymondham

The Man

As I skidded around the corner, I saw him. My body paralysed into a statue and my feet felt too heavy. He came closer, close enough that I could feel the heat of his breath. My eyes were scorched by the sight of his horrific mask, blood was dripping from the eye holes. He started to move closer, he reached his wrinkly, bony hand up to my face and, with that, I turned around and ran. I met the end of a bricked tunnel. There was nothing. I screamed until my lungs were sore. I cried until I was ended.

Amelia Gorvin (13)
Wymondham High Academy, Wymondham

Run

Nowhere is safe now they know about it, they will come. It was 1988, my friend and I just found out, we had to stop them. We stole what they wanted and for four years, hid and ran before it happened. We were hiding in an abandoned resistance facility. I was looking at plans for a nuke that would decimate everything in a two-hundred-mile radius. That was when it happened. My friend screamed, then went as limp as a ragdoll. He had a bullet in his head. I had no time to mourn. I had to leave. Now!

Joshua Hanton (11)

Wymondham High Academy, Wymondham

Never Alone

Sirens screamed through my ears. They were above and all around me. I could feel it. I started to run, not knowing where I was going. Not knowing where I was coming from. My heart was pounding out of my chest. I was shaking uncontrollably. My head was spinning but my legs just carried me. I always thought I was a weak runner but the trees were passing me like cars on a motorway. I thought I lost them, the police. You would never know it, you were alone with them nearby. I was not alone anymore.

Bronwen Nelson (11)
Wymondham High Academy, Wymondham

Hide-And-Seek

I couldn't run for much longer before I had to stop and hide. I was close to a forest where I could hide and he would never find me. I ran like lightning to save my life from this terrifying creature. I didn't have much time to hide before he came searching for me. Five minutes later, I heard the screeching sirens. That meant the creature was out in the wild. I heard footsteps coming closer to me as I held my breath and hid behind a tree. I peeked from the side and tripped. He saw me...

Alina Ciausu (12)
Wymondham High Academy, Wymondham

Escape Plan

The lights blinded me. All I could hear was a loud ringing. My legs were dead. I had escaped but I couldn't run for much longer. The pain was agony. At least if I was dead, the pain would be gone. I could feel the blood swirling in my mouth, drowning me. I didn't know what to do. That's when I realised this was the last minute for me.

Two hours earlier.

I was chained to a chair, my hands tied behind me. All I could see was a pitch-black room. I knew I had to escape before my death.

Ryan Shingfield (11)
Wymondham High Academy, Wymondham

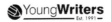

The Grand Plan Must Be Made!

I lie on the small, worn-out bed, wondering how I can escape. I have obviously tried to escape but it was never successful as I don't have a right arm. Funny thing, that was my dominant arm. I was fighting an army of aliens when my arm got stuck in the middle of two rocks. I tugged my arm but there was no hope so I had to amputate it. Unfortunately, the Intergalactic Space Police caught me. Here I am now. All I need is to get my robotic arm from the vault. This time, I'm going to escape!

Devadutt Rajesh Nair (11)
Wymondham High Academy, Wymondham

The Purge

The sirens went off, the purge began. I knew I needed to run. I decided to hide in a school. I knew that no one would look in a school, they're boring. I heard squeaking. I looked out the window to see nine shady-looking figures coming straight towards me. I had to leave but how? Luckily, I was on the bottom floor so I jumped out of the window and hoped that no one would see me. I saw some weird things that day, rockets going off and more. Then I got my phone out and the purge was over.

Tyler Peters (13)
Wymondham High Academy, Wymondham

Caretaker

If you are reading this, it has happened again. Suddenly, I hear my only exit slam shut, the screaming lock as if the poor children who were massacred in this building were warning me to run. I didn't get a chance to finish the letter that was started. I heard walking up the stairs. I panicked and ran to the library, there the murderer stood with an axe. I screamed and began to run. He started to chase me in the massive house. I felt cold blood on my arm and realised that was it...

Tom Pestell (12)
Wymondham High Academy, Wymondham

I Became The Prey

I couldn't run for much longer. My legs were aching, it felt like I ran two hundred miles. I was out of breath and about to collapse when a light beamed on me. Then I heard gunshots. I knew they'd found me. It was the middle of the night, it was pitch-black. I looked back and saw the guards catching up with me. Suddenly, I banged into the gate and got an electric shock as I fell to the ground. I saw a light, it felt like a gigantic light. The shadow of the guard came over me...

Finley Statham (12)
Wymondham High Academy, Wymondham

On The Run!

I'm free? Now all I have to do is run for my life. I can hear the sirens shrieking, waiting to catch me once again. I'm not the fastest runner. My mind is clueless. Where do I hide? How long have I got 'til I am caught? I just follow the road, hoping it leads me to a place to hide. I turn the corner and throw myself in the bush. I can hear dogs sniffing me down. Are they going to catch me? I look up and there is a bright light. A helicopter! I've been caught for sure!

Sophie Anne Smith (12)
Wymondham High Academy, Wymondham

Hunted

My sister Nancy, her boyfriend Ed and I had gone for a short break to a local island. We had a few hours to pass before our parents were home so we decided to take a walk in the forest. Suddenly, two men jumped out of the bushes and dragged Ed away. We followed the men and we came across a small camp and saw skinned bodies hung from trees and spotted Ed being placed over an open fire. It was only then that we realised that they were going to cook Ed alive and eat him as their food.

Noah Lebidineuse
Wymondham High Academy, Wymondham

He...

They were close. He wanted me. I ran as fast as I could. I found myself in a forest. It was raining. I was so cold. My legs and arms were numb! I could hear sirens coming towards me. My legs felt stuck. I could not move them. I screamed for my life and then realised he was near me. *Bang!* I woke up in a dark, cold room with a light flickering. I could hear footsteps coming as a tear fell from my eye. I sat in the horrible room, waiting as my heart raced. Then he came in...

Austeja Kazemekaite (11)
Wymondham High Academy, Wymondham

Run

We had to leave. Now. He grabbed me by the neck as I held onto my life. I felt scared and thought I was gonna drop dead. He got out a gun while I sprinted for my life. He roared in anger as he followed me out the school gates while I ran and ran until I couldn't breathe or run any longer. I sat down in the deep, silent wood. He found me. He grabbed me by the neck, got out a gun and placed it onto my injured head. Then he went... *bang!* I was about to die.

Erica Holt (11)
Wymondham High Academy, Wymondham

Locked Away!

I had twenty-four hours left. I had to escape this room before it was too late. I tried every key but it was just not working.
Twenty-three hours left until it was the end of my life. I was close to getting out but it just wasn't working. I had to find a key so I could get out before it was too late.
I had only six hours left, I had to find this key but I just couldn't find it anywhere. All of a sudden, I found it in one of the boxes. I was lucky!

Ellie-Rose O'Brien (12)
Wymondham High Academy, Wymondham

Death Within The Star

I'm lost... I'm tired... I'm hunted. I cannot believe that this star I used to adore is now the reason that I may not make it through the day. I know they are coming for me. I knew as soon as my Papa screamed for me to get out and I saw some huge men at the door. My heart beats faster with every step, leaping every time I see someone. I try to cover my star, no one can see, no one can know. I know I will die soon. Even if I live, it will be in fear.

Tilly Butler (12)
Wymondham High Academy, Wymondham

The Attack On Earth

I had to go, it knew I was here. It would hunt me and kill me like everyone else. I ran but I knew it was no use and it would catch up and murder me in seconds. The guilt of not being able to save my family weighed me down. I couldn't keep running, I had to fight it. I hid in a bush and waited. I thought about how many people were alive. It jumped out at me and that was the last thing I remembered. I was in a strange place with others who survived the shadow.

Freddie Lambert (12)
Wymondham High Academy, Wymondham

YOUNG WRITERS INFORMATION

We hope you have enjoyed reading this book – and that you will continue to in the coming years.

If you're a young writer who enjoys reading and creative writing, or the parent of an enthusiastic poet or story writer, do visit our website **www.youngwriters.co.uk**. Here you will find free competitions, workshops and games, as well as recommended reads, a poetry glossary and our blog. There's lots to keep budding writers motivated to write!

If you would like to order further copies of this book, or any of our other titles, then please give us a call or order via your online account.

Young Writers
Remus House
Coltsfoot Drive
Peterborough
PE2 9BF
(01733) 890066
info@youngwriters.co.uk